STAR CROSSED

ARIES RISING

BONNIE HEARN HILL

RP|TEENS
PHILADELPHIA • LONDON

Library of Congress Control Number: 2009940138

ISBN 978-0-7624-3670-5

Cover and interior design by Ryan Hayes
Typography: Chronicle Text, Knockout, Affair
Cover Photo: iStock

Published by Running Press Teens, an imprint of
Running Press Book Publishers
2300 Chestnut Street
Philadelphia, PA 19103-4371

Visit us on the web!
www.runningpress.com

To the Fridays, with much love and gratitude:
Ryan Booth, Hazel Dixon-Cooper,
Dennis C. Lewis, Sheree Petree,
and Christopher Allen Poe.

What's your sign?
Check out ours.

Chili, actually Jessica Chiliderian, one of my two best friends, a talkative, generous **Gemini**, and the beauty among us. Geminis talk (and talk and talk), but Geminis can also care. I believe she does, and she'll soon have a chance to prove it.

Paige, my other BFF, the class brain and soon-to-be fashion designer. She's totally capable of surprising anyone who would dare to write her off as just another daydreaming **Pisces**. Sure, the Fish can get lost in the sea of dreams, but not this one, especially not now.

Nathan, a hot, show-stopping **Leo**, the center of everyone's attention, especially mine. And did I mention *hot*? That golden Lion will always be on stage, with or without his mane.

Geneva, the way-too-popular editor of our school paper. This senior's the embodiment of **Libra** indecision, which she would call *balance,* not to mention big-time manipulation, which she would call *fairness.* Now if I can just keep her away from Nathan—and everything else I want.

Frankenstein, Mr. Franklin, if I'm going to be respectful. English teacher, stubborn **Taurus** with a fondness for food and a nagging reminder about what he calls *honest writing.* This recently divorced, not-too-happy guy holds the key to whether or not

I get the summer fellowship to California State University at Monterey Bay.

Charles, a sweet, shy **Cancer** who's terrified of Frankenstein. If true to Moonchild form, he's ruled by emotion. What is it about him that always makes me feel so sad?

The Gears of War, signs unknown, but I'm betting on fire. A secret group of guys who named themselves after a video game. Their disturbing pranks are striking way too close to home. If I can figure out who they are, I'll win Frankenstein's respect and maybe a great deal more.

Trevor, a secretive **Scorpio** jock, he seems as hot for Chili as she is for him. Except for that nasty little Scorpio habit of clinging to the past. In Trevor's life, that past is spelled K-A-T.

Kat, cute, outgoing **Aries** cheerleader and Trevor's kind-of ex, known for getting what she wants and creating huge, nasty scenes when she doesn't. Aries is cardinal fire, used to taking charge. And Kat intends to.

Ms. Snider, our cool **Capricorn** journalism teacher with a secret admirer. Or is it two? Always elegant, this Capricorn may be too busy trying to get ahead to smell the roses. But she hasn't counted on the evil Gears invading her life.

Mom, the famous **Sagittarius,** who's out there achieving her dream. As proud as I am of her, I wish this travel- and change-loving Sadge could have both a career and a hands-on home life.

Dad, Virgo artist, working for an ad agency, detail-oriented (make that obsessive-compulsive) and a bit frugal (make that cheap). Left in charge of me while Mom's on the road, he's got to be as lonely as I am.

And me, **Logan McRae, Aquarian,** trying to save the world, the same as most who share my sign. *Too detached,* some astrologers (and Frankenstein) would say. But I'm attempting to put more of *me* into my essay assignments. Once I identify the Gears and write about the experience, even Frankenstein will take notice. The odds were stacked against me until I discovered *Fearless Astrology.* Now that the book is in my hands, it's a whole new game.

NO ONE NEED FEAR THE STARS. THEY DON'T LIMIT OUR
DESTINY, ONLY POINT OUT POSSIBILITIES. INDEED,
THE STARS, THE PLANETS, AND THE VERY STUDY OF
THE ZODIAC CAN TRANSFORM OUR LIVES.

—Fearless Astrology

It started with a wish. That's all I was doing that day, wishing my life were different, wishing Geneva Hamilton didn't have such a cute butt, wishing Nathan would look at me the way he looked at her. And most of all, wishing that Frankenstein thought enough of my writing to recommend me for the California State University at Monterey Bay fellowship.

It was a cool April afternoon in Terra Bella Beach, California, the way it gets in early spring just before the sun breaks through the clouds. Paige and I had begged Chili to put the top down anyway. No other kid at Terra High had a new Mitsubishi Spyder convertible, in liquid silver, no less. But then no other kid had Andy Chiliderian of *Andy C's Motors* for a dad.

As we drove home, Chili and Paige tried to talk me out of my foul mood.

"You can make up the grade, Logan." Chili's hair, a mass of highlights, whipped around her face, even though she'd clipped it back. "And Nathan's not worth worrying about."

"Easy for you to say," I told her. "He said he was into me. We actually kissed after the dance last week."

"Which just proves how lucky you are to be rid of the jerk. Am I right, Paige?"

"Right." Paige leaned forward, and the beaded fringe of her poncho slammed into the back of my neck. "If all he cares about is a great body . . ."

"Then he's like every other guy, right?"

We all knew that my curly auburn hair and stick-straight build was no match for Geneva Hamilton's amazing blond self. And we had all seen that amazing blond self leaning against Nathan Sullivan's Honda hybrid after school. He hadn't even looked up when we drove past. Whatever fleeting *something* I had imagined happening between Nathan and me was over.

"Why don't you have dinner at my house?" The look of pity that flashed across Chili's face actually made me feel worse. "Mom made extra shish kebab for you and your dad. You might as well eat it with us. He'll probably be working late again."

Everyone knew my dad worked late at the ad agency. Everyone knew my mom was on tour. Not even my two best friends had any idea how lonely I was with this arrangement.

"I should just go home," I said.

"Come on, Logan. You know Mom would love to have you."

"Tell Stella I said thanks, but I can't."

"Why not?" Chili asked.

"I have to finish the next English essay by Wednesday. *A moment that changed my life.* How impossible is that? I have no idea what to write."

"Can you believe how much work Frankenstein is piling on us this year?" Chili made a face. "I bet you already finished yours, didn't you, Paige?"

"Last weekend," Paige said. "Do you want me to help you guys? I have lots of leftover quotations from my research."

"Why not?" Chili glanced over at me. "You're not going to pass up an offer like that, are you? Put the English grade and the broken heart on hold tonight."

"Would you feel the same way if it was Trevor looking at Geneva like that?" I asked.

"Trevor would never." She hit the brake as we approached a red light. "Of course, he's never looked at *me* like that either."

"But you know he will. He and Kat only just broke up."

"He won't. Kat's a cheerleader, and I'm only—"

"Only perfect," I finished for her.

She was the star of our small circle, the one with the rich

dad and the full-time mother. The beautiful one.

Although Chili constantly complained that she looked "too Armenian," Stella always said there would be no nose jobs under her roof. Not that Chili needed any cosmetic enhancement. The nose balanced her perfect, zit-free face and huge, expressive eyes.

Paige and I were the nerds, although Paige's nerd-dom resulted from shyness, a need to please, and a reputation as the class brain. Her pale lashes were almost invisible. Blue eyes blurred behind her glasses.

Her true personality, the real Paige, was reflected only in the bizarre fashions she designed. The multicolored beaded poncho that had smacked my head not long before was what my gram would call "far-out."

I'd admired Paige's wild creations since first grade and even let her talk me into wearing some of them now and then. I'd never let her talk me into glasses, though. From an early age, I memorized eye charts. *O-T-F-U-Y. C-Z-L-D-T.* I'm hoping someday soon there will be a laser surgery that fixes complex astigmatisms like mine. In the meantime, it's amazing how well you can get by if you squint and tilt your head.

That intense gaze of mine might be the reason people said my hazel eyes were my best feature. Or it might be that it's the only compliment they could think of. If not for conditioner, my long hair would resemble straw the color of autumn leaves. And I could work my glutes for the rest of my life and never have a butt like Geneva's.

Paige had done our homework in grade school and later coached us to do it ourselves. As much as I wanted to go home alone and stuff myself with Ben & Jerry's Chunky Monkey, I needed all the help she could give.

Chili insisted that we stop at her house to pick up the food Stella had prepared for my dad and me, and then she drove me home. We all headed inside to get a start on the English assignment.

Being with them made the house feel less lonely. We ended up in the computer room my dad and I shared—my nursery in its past life.

"How can you work in here?" Chili asked. "It's so cluttered."

That was what I liked about the room. I could imagine how it must look to her, though, with my dad's art table wedged in a corner and the stack of plastic storage boxes spilling out of the closet beside it.

"Want to go back to my bedroom instead?" I asked. "The laptop's in there."

"This is fine. Actually, I kind of like its weirdness." Her gaze shifted to the closet. "What's in those boxes?"

"Just a bunch of old stuff."

She went over and peered at a label. "This one says *Tuscany*."

"My folks did a lot of traveling before I was born. They went everywhere, all six continents."

"Seven," Paige corrected.

"Antarctica," I said. "I always forget."

Both of them were studying the assortment of boxes in the closet.

"Hey, what's this?" Chili tapped her nails against the top of my mom's ebony chest.

I walked over to it, knelt down on the floor, and lifted the lid.

"Cool," Chili said, and moved closer. "Look, Paige. There's all kinds of yearbooks and pictures in here."

"Is that a golf trophy?" Paige asked.

I reached for the glint of gold and pulled it out.

"Only from college. It's all pretty boring," I mumbled, then replaced the trophy and started to close the box. This was my mother's past. It didn't have much to do with me and had nothing to do with my friends.

That was when I saw it. An old black, leather-bound book with a sprinkling of silver stars, tarnished now, on its cover.

I yanked it out. *Fearless Astrology* by J. Blair.

"Come on," Chili said. "We should get started."

I couldn't take my eyes off the book, could only stare at the words on the cover. *Transform Your Life with Astrology.* My hands trembled. If anyone needed transforming, I did.

"What's that?" Chili demanded. "What's that book?"

"Nothing." I held it close, the stars pressing against my chest, so that she and Paige couldn't see the title. Then, carefully, I placed it back in the box. "Now, if it's okay with you, Paige, I need all the help I can get on this essay for Frankenstein."

NOTES TO SELF

The book says—all right, make that advises—that I keep a record of my *Fearless Astrology* experience. Since I don't have any experience yet, there's not much I can write here in my journal. There's a lot I can hope for, though. If *Fearless Astrology* really can change my life, what would I want? The Monterey Fellowship for Outstanding High School Student Writers. That's a no-brainer. And if I get another wish, well, of course, there's always Nathan. Okay, *Fearless Astrology*. I'm going to give you a try.

YOUR FIRST STEP TOWARD FEARLESS ASTROLOGY IS
IDENTIFYING YOUR SUN SIGN. IT IS THE ESSENCE OF
YOUR CHARACTER.

—*Fearless Astrology*

could hardly wait for Paige and Chili to leave so that I could start reading the astrology book. By the time my dad got home, he was tired from working late and distracted by the covered plate of pilaf and shish kebab that Stella had made. Even with the dark circles beneath his hazel eyes, he was still one of the most handsome men I'd ever seen. Part of it was his thick reddish-brown hair that had never known a blow-dryer and fell across his brow as if the wind had plastered it there, which tonight it probably had. The rest was the quiet, thoughtful way he spoke, as if the person he was addressing—in this case me—was the most important human in the world.

"Join me?" he asked, and lifted the foil from the plate.

"I already had some."

"Then just keep me company while I eat. Unless you're busy with homework."

"Actually, I was working on something for Mr. Franklin's class."

Not a lie. If the book helped me figure out Frankenstein, it would be more valuable than any homework assignment I could be doing.

"Good for you." He set himself a place at the counter.

I eased my way out of the kitchen, then headed down the hall to my room.

The book was almost four hundred pages long and loaded with advice. I didn't know where to start. With Sun signs, I decided. Moon signs looked more complicated, and rising signs, Mars, Venus, and the rest of them were over my head. So, okay, Sun signs.

According to what I read, your Sun sign is your basic character, your Moon is your emotional structure, and your Rising sign is they way you're perceived. I looked up Nathan's Sun sign first. He was a Leo.

I already knew I was an Aquarius, a sign I shared with Oprah Winfrey, Abraham Lincoln, and Lauren Conrad. A sign that wanted to save the world. Well, maybe someday. First I had to save myself, not to mention get to the summer class in Monterey and forget that Nathan had ever mattered to me.

We'd never been out together, and that delicious, lingering

kiss in the school parking lot after the dance had seemed to surprise him as much as it did me. That wasn't exactly a commitment, and according to *Fearless Astrology*, commitment wouldn't be Nathan's most pressing need anyway.

No. That most pressing need would be being on stage 24/7.

"The Leo male shines in the spotlight," the book said. "He's easily won over by attention and flattery."

Attention and flattery. Could something that simple really make Nathan interested in me again? I wasn't even sure how to flatter a guy who obviously already had a high opinion of himself. But lacking Geneva's arsenal of natural gifts, I was willing to try. Now if only I knew Frankenstein's sign, I might figure out a way to get the fellowship.

I barely slept at all that night, and when my alarm went off, I realized that I was still propped up in bed, and the book was in my lap. It was all I could do to get to English class on time.

When I walked in, Frankenstein was bragging to the class about how many bicep curls he'd done that morning. What teacher talks to his students about his biceps? He wore a pale blue polo shirt the same color as his eyes. Even though he was in his early thirties, his dark hair was longer than any of the other male teachers'. His addiction to weight training and attachment to his restored Corvette were legendary. So was his abrasive personality. He'd already chastised two other students before he focused his attention on me.

"Hey, McRae," he said. "Saw your mom on television this weekend."

Every head in the classroom turned to look at me.

"I hear she won," I replied.

"You *hear*?" He gave me a look that made me cringe. "You didn't talk to your own mom?"

"I was asleep when she spoke with my dad."

Before class was over, he'd insulted most of us and terrified the others.

"Bellamy, you contribute nothing to this class," he roared at poor Charles, the last kid who needed to be harassed.

"What do you want?" Charles's reedy voice sounded as timid as he looked.

"I want you to take part, that's all." He looked past Charles's shoulder and shifted his watery blue eyes to me. "You too, McRae. Part of your grade in here is based on class participation, you know."

I wanted to say that I did speak up in class. I just didn't like the personal questions that Frankenstein was so good at asking.

I said nothing, just stared across the desks at Charles. He met my eyes for the first time since I'd known him and gave me a weak smile. The only other times I'd seen him do that was when Ms. Snider talked to him in journalism class.

Just then, the bell rang. With a final look at me, Charles bolted out of the room. I forced myself to stay seated.

Once the room was empty, I got up and approached Frankenstein's desk. He studied me with narrowed eyes.

"I do try to contribute, Mr. Franklin." I forced myself to

speak clearly. "I hope you won't mark me down for not participating just because I don't like discussing personal stuff."

"You mean your mom? Well, I happen to be a golf fan." He squinted as if looking into the sun. Hangover, I thought. Chili's dad said he spent a lot of time at the bar across the street from the dealership. "She's a celebrity, your mom. You should be proud of her."

"I am proud," I said, then went ahead with the little speech I'd hatched that morning. It was a complete lie, but I could sell Ms. Snider on the idea later if he agreed. "Ah, I'm writing a story for the school paper, and I'd like to interview you. So would you mind telling me when you were born?"

"You need my birth date for a story?" He might as well have said a *stupid* story.

"I thought it might be a different slant."

He crossed his arms over his burly frame. "I know what you're up to. You just want to know how old I am."

What an egomaniac. I sighed. "You don't have to tell me the year you were born. I just thought it might be fun to include your astrological sign in the article, that's all."

"That's all you want? My birthday? Okay, then. It's Cinco de Mayo. That's all you're getting out of me, though."

"May fifth?" I'd learned that much in first-year Spanish.

He nodded. "That's right."

"Thanks."

I had what I needed now. And soon I'd know the rest.

As I left his class, I saw Nathan coming from the cafeteria.

Although the book said most Leos can be spotted by their thick manes, Nathan was bald. He'd shaved off his hair for a Kids and Cancer benefit.

He appeared to be trying to decide whether or not to speak. I remembered what the book said about Leos. *Attention and flattery*. I'd always preferred to remain quiet and analyze a situation before speaking up—Aquarius trait, I realized now. This time, I forced myself to smile.

"Hi, Nathan."

"Hey." He seemed to relax, no doubt relieved that I hadn't started in on him about Geneva.

"Love the shaved head," I told him. "You should keep it that way."

"You really think so?"

I studied those eyes, almost turquoise, those lips that had pressed into mine after the dance. "For sure. It makes you stand out."

"Oh, yeah?" His eyes narrowed, and I knew he was wondering if I was going to bring up Geneva. "You think I need to stand out?"

"Well, you mentioned that you were going to audition for the school play. Looking a little different might be a plus."

"Let's hope. Frankenstein's directing, and I'm not exactly his favorite person."

Just think, both of our destinies depended on one teacher. Even though it wasn't that unusual in a school as small as ours, it still gave us something in common.

"He's not liking anyone lately," I said, in a voice more confident than I would ever be. "When it comes down to it, though, he'll have to give you the part. There's no one in school as talented as you are. Everyone knows that, even him."

Heat flooded my cheeks. The blatant flattery made me feel like a total fake. Nathan seemed to bask in it, though, just as the book said.

"Well, thanks, Logan."

Might as well go all out. "You could be an actor if you wanted to be," I said. "Maybe even a star."

"I've thought about it, but that would send my mom straight back to therapy."

He grinned as if it were a joke, so I just smiled. "Well, let me know what happens with the play."

"I'll do that." He leaned down, let his lips graze my ear. "Maybe give you a call this weekend?"

"Sure." My cheeks had to be scarlet now. "Just remember what I said. You'll get the part."

I watched him walk away, astounded that I had mustered the nerve to pull off that encounter. Not to mention that it might actually have worked.

Chili stood across the corridor from me in leggings and a deep burgundy tunic, grinning. How long had she been there? She must have seen the whole thing.

I hurried over to her and knew that the victory must be plastered all over my face.

"Nathan looks kind of into you," she whispered. "What did you do to him?"

I shook my head. "Don't even ask," I told her. "You'd never believe it."

NOTES TO SELF

I'm trying to stay calm right now, but I must admit that after one day, I'm starting to like this zodiac stuff. No, that's not true. I am hopelessly, passionately obsessed with it. When Nathan looked at me like that, I realized that I might just have something Geneva doesn't. And if it works on Nathan, it just might work on Frankenstein too. His committee is in charge of picking the three fellowship finalists, and we'll each submit a writing sample to the committee. On June 1, the winner will be announced. It's going to come down to hard work, a lot of luck, and who knows? Maybe a little *Fearless Astrology*?

A MOMENT THAT CHANGED MY LIFE

Logan McRae

1st draft

I see a television screen, women swinging golf clubs into a sea of green. I'm very young, maybe five or so, barely old enough to understand that there is something wrong. My mother sits beside me on the sofa. Her body is rigid, and when I look up, I realize that tears are coming from her eyes. No sound, only tears. I want to make them stop, but I don't know how. Her gaze and her pain are focused on those women on the screen.

"So unfair," she whispers. "I'm better than all of them."

As if remembering me, she says, "Sorry, sweetie," pats my leg, and goes back to glaring at the television. I know then that she wants to be where those women are and not here with me. I may even guess that one day she will be. But I don't say anything. Like her, I don't make a sound.

There is no way I can turn this in to Frankenstein. Better try again.

A MOMENT THAT CHANGED MY LIFE

Logan McRae

Final draft

Many moments shape our lives. Only tragedy or amazing joy can change them. It is impossible to live without change. As Heraclitus wrote, "All is flux; nothing stays still."

My grandmother's generation was changed by the assassination of John Fitzgerald Kennedy. My generation was changed by the events of September 11, 2001.

I learned from that tragedy how very rapidly life as we know it can spin out of control. Eric Hoffer wrote, "In times of change, learners inherit the Earth, while the learned find themselves beautifully equipped to deal with a world that no longer exists."

I believe that change is less about what actually happens to us, and more about what we learn from it.

Darn. Why did the final draft sound so dead?

3

TAURUS (APRIL 20–21 TO MAY 20–21) IS STABLE, STUBBORN, AND SENSUOUS, ESPECIALLY WHEN IT COMES TO THE APPRECIATION AND CONSUMPTION OF FOOD AND OTHER PLEASURES. HE IS THE GREAT BULL, USUALLY PLACID AND COMMITTED TO FAIRNESS, BUT WHEN TAUNTED, ANGRY, EVEN DANGEROUS.

—Fearless Astrology

Taurus. Sign of Bono, George Clooney, Miranda Cosgrove, and Malcolm X.

Frankenstein was a Taurus. With that broad chest of his, he actually looked like a bull. Even though I was the only one at home, I locked myself in my room with the book. Why had Mr. Franklin become such an angry Bull lately? Maybe it had something to do with his divorce. I'd learned that tidbit from Paige, whose aunt worked in the school's admin office.

Like it or not, he was the most important person in my life right now, equally as important as Nathan. No, even more than Nathan. With a top grade in his class and a written recommendation, I'd have a good chance of making the top three, and if my final writing sample was strong enough, I'd be spending the summer in Monterey's creative writing program for outstanding high school journalism students. How could I explain to him that this was the greatest dream of my life? It was what becoming a fashion designer was to Paige, what getting a degree in business was to Chili, and what being a golfer was to my mom.

I was willing to work hard and earn his respect. Would that be enough to appeal to the Taurus sense of fairness?

I kept reading. The Bull liked nature. He was attracted to wealth, food, and *sensuous pursuits*, which I was starting to figure out meant sex. Disgusting. I didn't want to think of my English teacher that way. Maybe I'd go the food route. Would my gram's cream cheese brownies qualify as sensuous? Would they get me the fellowship? Was this ridiculous? I was so desperate to try anything that I went shopping for chocolate chips.

T he minute I got out of Chili's car at school the next morning, I realized that the Gears of War had struck again.

SNIDER PUTS OUT was spray-painted in huge black letters across the window of the administration building. This was the worst act yet by the group of morons who'd been pulling stupid pranks for about a month now.

Chili gasped. "Can you believe it? They're getting braver. Last time they just stole mailboxes and dumped them in the pool."

As she spoke, two maintenance workers came around the corner with ladders.

"They're a little late," I said. "Everyone must have seen it."

"Do you think she does?" Chili whispered.

"Ms. Snider, you mean? Put out?"

She nodded. "Right."

"I don't know," I said, "but I'll bet everyone in this school is asking themselves that question right now."

At the end of Frankenstein's class, I approached his desk, handed him a foil-wrapped package, and said, "I can't eat my grandmother's brownies because I have a dental exam coming up." I didn't mention that my gram was on a cruise to Alaska or that I had baked the brownies myself the night before.

"What's this?" he roared before I could get out of the room.

"Dental exam," I repeated.

"I never took you for an apple polisher, McRae."

My face burned. Thank goodness everybody else had already left.

"I'm not," I said. "I just didn't know who else to give these to."

"You sure you didn't put anything in them?"

"Of course not." My voice sounded as miserable as I felt. "It was a dumb idea. I'm sorry." I reached out for the brownies.

He waved my hand away. "Not necessarily. I just wanted

to be sure of your motives."

"All right, then." I got out of there before he could change his mind or ask me any more questions.

By the time I got to Snider's journalism class, everyone was talking about the Gears and their latest victory.

Brooke Snider was the best-looking teacher in school, and probably the youngest. In spite of her turtlenecks and pantsuits, she was hot. Her hair, pulled up in the back, was parted in the middle with blond tendrils falling along each cheek. She wore light pink lipstick that was as close as you could get to gloss.

She was a fun teacher too, but not today. No, today I could tell that she was livid.

The room was arranged in six large tables, and the only one with a seat left was occupied by Charles Bellamy. I did not mind sitting with him, especially after what Frankenstein had put him through the day before. Besides, the table was the closest to the door, and I wanted to be as far away as possible from that look on Ms. Snider's face.

Geneva sat in front, of course, surrounded by the girls who idolized her. They shamelessly tried to copy everything from the way she dressed—understated and neutral—to the way she talked—slow, low, and musical. It was the way I imagined girls who attended private school spoke. Geneva didn't have friends; she had admirers. Kat, the manic cheerleader, was the only one who seemed to actually hang out with her.

A senior like Nathan, Geneva was almost his height, taller

than most of the guys, but well proportioned. And none of the boys seemed to worry too much about looking up to her. She walked around as if the rest of the girls at school were to blame for not being born as beautiful as she was. And to make it worse, she was smart.

"Logan." Her tone was sharp, and she motioned me to her desk.

I walked up slowly and hoped she didn't think that I was involved in any of what had happened this morning.

"Yes?"

"I understand you're writing an article about Mr. Franklin," she began, her voice low against the blanket of conversation behind us. "Why didn't you tell me that?"

Busted. Why hadn't I realized that teachers talked to each other? Even teachers as worlds apart as Snider and Frankenstein.

"I just kicked the idea around with him. I thought it might be interesting to do something from an astrological perspective. That's all."

She cocked her head, and I could see in her eyes that she was distracted. She must hate what was going on right now. "Do you know anything about astrology?"

"I've started studying it a little," I said.

"So it wasn't just a regular Feature Teacher article you were discussing with Mr. Franklin?" She looked relieved. "You do know, in either case, you'd have to get Geneva's approval. She's the editor, after all."

"I understand," I said. "I was thinking of maybe doing a series of astrological articles. If that's all right with you, of course."

"An astrology column?"

"It would just be for fun." My brain finally kicked in. "I could call it 'Star Crossed' and feature a different Sun sign in every issue."

She nodded, but I could see that her mind was still on the words written on the administration building.

"Sure, talk it over with Geneva, and we'll see." She paused then and looked more like her old self. "It's good that you're thinking of ways to improve the newspaper, Logan, but you shouldn't have spoken with Mr. Franklin until you ran it past Geneva and me."

"I'm sorry," I said. "We were talking, and it just kind of happened."

"It's fine, and your idea could be a workable one. I don't mean to discourage you."

"You could never discourage me." The words poured out of me before I could stop them. "You're a wonderful teacher."

"Thank you." Her bottom lip trembled. "You may take your seat now."

On the way to the parking lot after history class that afternoon, I had a text message on my phone. And not just any text message either.

are u busy friday?

My fingers trembled as I texted back.

sup?

The reply asked:

wanna hang?

"I don't believe it." My hands were shaking.

"What?" Chili demanded.

She and Paige moved closer. I looked up into their faces.

"I think Nathan just asked me out."

They screamed and wrapped their arms around me. In the parking lot, Geneva stalked right past us as if we didn't exist. Without her posse for once.

At that moment, all that mattered were those words on my phone. Nathan hadn't even waited until the weekend to get in touch with me. Could the advice in the astrology book actually be working?

ok, I texted back.

Okay being quite the understatement.

NOTES TO SELF

Can this be happening? I treat Nathan like a Leo and he asks me out? As much as I want to be skeptical, I'm just so excited. And if I can get him to notice me, there's got to be a way to get Frankenstein on my side. Please let Frankenstein like the brownies and transfer the like to me. I went with Paige tonight to buy fabric for some costumes she's making for the school play. She said that her aunt in the admin office told her Frankenstein was crushed by his divorce. That's the word she used. Come to think of it, he kind of looks that way. I need to find a way to un-crush him if I'm going to be one of the finalists for the fellowship.

WHILE THE SUN REPRESENTS YOUR CONSCIOUS PUR-
POSE IN LIFE, THE MOON IS THE KEY TO THE DEEPER
EMOTIONAL SELF. IT'S WHERE YOUR SECRETS AND
DESIRES LIVE. REVIEW THE CHART, THEN TAKE THE
FOLLOWING TEST TO GET IN TOUCH WITH YOUR MOON.

—Fearless Astrology

Moon sign Self-Test

Your Sun sign: *Aquarius*
Your Moon sign: *Pisces*
Most positive Moon aspect: *Nurturing others.*
Most hindering Moon aspect: *Too shy about my own
needs. I don't know how to ask for what I want or express my
feelings. Why?*
How your Moon can help transform your life:
Aquarius is a thinking sign; Pisces is a feeling sign. Maybe I

need to do less thinking and more feeling. Maybe I shouldn't be so scared to feel. Maybe I'm spending too much time taking this stupid test.

—Logan McRae

It was crazy to think that something as remote as the position of the moon could have an effect on my personality. I went to the chart in the back of the book and highlighted my birth year. I was born on the day before Valentine's, which I already knew made me an Aquarius. That meant I had a Pisces Moon, which I hadn't known. The description in the book seemed to fit, and most of the others didn't. If my Moon were in Gemini, for instance, I would talk a lot more than I did, like Chili. If it were in Scorpio, I'd talk a lot less, crave more solitude. I needed to figure out Nathan's Moon.

He checked in again after I got home from school.

Hows yur day

Boooring—hows yurs? I replied.

lonely

whats wrong? I asked.

Nothing—can't wait til Friday—later

That's all he wrote, but it was enough. I really was getting a second chance at him.

The soft sunlight of the day had been blotted out by storm clouds, but I felt warm all over. I'd get through the journalism open house that night and count the minutes until Friday. I was not excited about the open house. It was probably going to be another Snider love fest about Geneva's editorial ability.

Might as well get out the Juicy Couture coat my mom gave me for my birthday back in February, the last time she'd been home for more than a night or a weekend. Its elegant blue-and-gray pattern seemed to calm the wildness of my hair. I put it on over leggings and a long top. Not bad, I had to admit.

I showed up at the open house feeling extra lame in my dad's minivan, its interior splattered with paint. Everyone else would be with their parents. And, yes, my dad would have taken off early if I'd asked, but I didn't feel right doing so since he'd only have to work that much later tomorrow night.

Fortunately, nobody noticed me drive up. The rain hadn't started yet. Stragglers from baseball practice drifted into the parking lot. They milled around, talking quietly in the dim light like members of a private club.

I spotted Trevor, his wavy light brown hair smashed down under a baseball cap. He was with J.T. Malone, also a senior, the tallest guy on the team, and Geneva's younger brother, Jared. Between the two tall guys, dark-haired J.T. and blond Jared, Trevor looked like a little boy. I got a glimpse of what Chili saw in him.

Drama tryouts were letting out as well. Kids in wigs and weird costumes drifted past the clusters of baseball players.

As I got out of the van and stepped into the parking lot, I heard the familiar "Hi, honey."

There stood Stella and Chili. In spite of the obvious age difference, they were dressed like sisters. Stella wore patterned rain boots and a parka with a leopard design. Chili's tapered pants ended in fuzzy Uggs.

School rules forbade everything from spaghetti straps to colored shoelaces. Chili wore both, no doubt on purpose. The shoelaces tied back her highlighted hair. The spaghetti straps peeked from beneath a wraparound gray wool jacket.

"You guys didn't have to come," I said. "It's no big deal."

"We wanted to, honey." Stella's smile was so warm and supportive that I felt like hugging her.

"Besides, I thought maybe T would be around," Chili said under her breath.

I waited until Stella headed out of the parking lot toward the classroom and whispered, "He was here."

"T? Where?"

"Right over there with the other baseball guys. I saw him just a minute or two ago."

"What are you waiting for?" she asked. "Let's go find him."

"I have to go inside. I promised Snider."

"It will just take a minute. Come on, Logan. Please."

How could I refuse? "Okay," I said. "But let's hurry."

We started down the corridor, past a bunch of other kids

and Jillian Berry, this outrageous art teacher with carrot-colored curls.

"Hey, Logan." Ms. Berry gave me a little wave in passing. "Tell Mac I said hi."

I winced at her use of my dad's nickname but waved back anyway.

"How does she know your dad?" Chili asked.

"It's a small town," I said. "All of the artists know one another."

"Some artist." She raised an eyebrow, and we giggled. Everyone knew that Berry specialized in painting men without faces—or clothes.

Dina Coulter turned the corner and headed toward us with lips curved into a perpetual valentine smile. Short, with dark hair, she could be cheerleader Kat's loser sister. Except that her only extracurricular activity seemed to be walking the halls and saying hello to everyone whose name she knew. In a school as small as ours, that was pretty much everybody.

"Hi, Logan," she said. "Hi, Chili."

We said our hellos and were almost to the journalism classroom when Chili stopped suddenly. "Oh, no. Look who's coming."

As nearsighted as I was, I could make out the shape of Frankenstein barreling down the hall from the direction of the drama classroom.

"McRae," he boomed before I could begin to think about where to hide. "Those brownies. They were awesome." He gave me a thumbs-up.

I cringed, wondering who else had seen the gesture and how relentlessly I'd be teased tomorrow.

"Thanks," I squeaked.

He was right in front of us now. The expression on his face was his version of friendly, I guessed. In spite of the cool weather, he wore a short-sleeved black polo shirt pulled tight across his thick chest.

"Regardless of your motive, cream-cheese brownies are my favorite. How'd you know?"

I could feel Chili's piercing stare, and I knew that she'd be demanding an explanation. "I didn't," I said, "but I'm glad you liked them."

"So, where are you heading? The journalism open house?"

Frankenstein was actually trying to have a normal conversation with me.

"Yes," I said. "We were just—"

"Isn't that starting right now?" He looked at his watch. "Come on. We'd better hurry."

We?

I glanced at Chili for direction, but all I got was a look of pure confusion.

"Meet you there in a few," she muttered.

Without another word, I hurried to keep up with him.

The overpowering scent of fruit punch filled the room. Was it my imagination, or did everyone turn to look at us when we entered?

Stella hurried over. "Where's Jessica?"

She never called Chili by her nickname.

"She's coming." I looked from her to Frankenstein, then back again. "Have you met Mr. Franklin, Stella?"

"It's a pleasure." She put out a manicured hand with its French pink-and-white acrylics. Together we moved to the front of the room.

A couple of dads in suits walked around shaking hands with the teachers. The principal and vice principal were also there. The rest were pretty much moms. The tables had been pushed together, and examples of the newspaper in various stages were spread across them. Guests moved around the tables sipping Styrofoam cups of punch and chatting. Most of the kids hung out on the sidelines. Not far from me, Charles Bellamy stood next to a bald older man in a suit. I gave him a little wave, and he nodded.

Sol Jackson, a huge, kind-of-cute junior who'd moved here last year, rushed in late, wearing a tie and spouting "Yes Ma'ams" to anyone he encountered. The guy was both clueless and smart, and he'd been the newspaper editor in his freshman year in Texas. Air sign all the way, maybe Gemini. If he kept up the charming talk, he'd be the newspaper editor after Geneva graduated. An improvement for sure.

Geneva's brother, Jared, stood in back with J.T. and Geneva's gorgeous, tall, platinum-haired mother, a model in her past life. I smiled at Jared, who'd always have a special place in my heart since he was the first boy I'd ever kissed.

He grinned back. Geneva's dad stood with her. Even though her parents were divorced and not speaking, both showed up for every school event. I felt a twinge of envy. *Yuck.* I still wished my mom could come just once.

The principal welcomed the guests. A city councilman gave a brief speech about what a fine school this was and what an outstanding journalism department we had. I wondered what Chili was doing and hoped she was having more fun than I was. Finally, Ms. Snider walked up to the podium. Her off-white pantsuit glowed like a pearl in the harsh light. I wondered how many guys were fantasizing about her *putting out.*

No doubt most of the people in this room were wondering if there was any truth to that spray-painted message. Although she had to be aware of that, she was poised as always. A gold trophy sat on her desk. From where I stood, I could only see a blur of the inscription.

"Producing a newspaper, whether a monthly, weekly, or daily, for a city or a school like this, is a major job," she said. "To place first in the talented field of all high schools in Terra Bella County is every school newspaper advisor's dream. That dream came true last year, and it's coming true again. For the second year in a row, we've placed first. Geneva Hamilton is our talented editor. Gen, please come on up here and accept this award."

Geneva strolled to the front, a smirk plastered across her lovely face. She wore khaki pants, a pale suede jacket, and matching low-pulled hat that covered most of her short blond hair.

When you're beautiful beyond belief, almost six feet tall, have fabulous boobs, and the best butt in California, you own the world. Every eye was on Geneva. The buzz of converstion stopped.

She took the trophy in both hands. "Thanks for this," she said. Then, with a look around the room, she added. "The newspaper is my passion, and I am willing to put in as much time as it takes to make it what it is and all it can be. This award is my motivation to continue producing the best high school paper in the county, the state, and maybe the country."

Not a mention of those of us on the staff. Not even any credit for Snider.

Her words were followed by more applause, most of it generated by Kat. Little brother Jared stepped forward and snapped a photo or two.

"What about us?" I realized Sol Jackson had moved beside me.

"Good question," I told him.

Finally, I could leave. I was so ready.

As I neared the door, Chili burst in.

"Look who I found." Her large eyes gleamed. "They're going to give us a ride home."

Trevor and Nathan stood behind her. Trevor was still in his practice uniform. Nathan was in a black sweater and jeans. His head was freshly shaved.

He smiled at me as if I were the best thing he'd seen all day or night.

"Does that work for you?" he asked.

"Sounds like fun," I managed to reply.

I was going to be with Nathan. Chili could drive me back to my hideous van later. To think that I hadn't wanted to come tonight.

Just then, Stella appeared. "I'm Mrs. Chiliderian," she said, and swept her Armenian mama gaze over the boys. "That's great you're giving my girls a ride home. See you at the house."

"Thanks, Mom." Chili turned from her and bestowed one of her most dazzling smiles on a clearly zoned Trevor. Smitten, is the way my gram would have described the look on his face. "Come on," Chili told him. "Before she changes her mind."

They rushed out of the room. Stella followed a few steps behind.

That left Nathan and me.

"Ready?" He said it as if we were on our way to a great adventure.

Thank you, astrology book. Thank you.

It was so much easier dealing with Nathan as a Leo than Nathan as a boy. Whatever I had done was working.

"Ready." I didn't dare turn back to see if Geneva was watching.

We were almost to the car when I heard some kind of commotion back on campus. Raised voices, shouts.

"What's that?" Nathan asked.

"I don't know." Chili grinned at Trevor, who gazed back at her as if hypnotized. "Want to go back?"

Just then, the night settled into silence again.

"Whatever it was is over now," Trevor said. "Let's get out of here."

We hurried to the car as the first drops of rain began to fall.

Nathan opened the passenger door in front.

"Hurry," he said, "before it really starts pouring."

I took his hand and let him help me inside. His arm slid around my shoulders and pulled me to him. I gazed up into those startling eyes. He bent down and brushed his lips across mine.

"Stop!"

Just then, a figure darted across the parking lot. It was Kat, Trevor's girlfriend until recently, and she was rushing toward us, short black hair plastered to her head.

"You don't waste any time, do you, you two-timer?"

"Kat, please." Trevor got out of the car, and was in such a hurry that he knocked off his baseball cap.

"Please what?" Kat ground her heel into it. "Don't embarrass you in front of your friends? Is that all you care about?"

Trevor leaned into the open door. "Sorry," he said to Chili. "I should deal with this."

Then he closed the door and started across the parking lot, Kat following. He didn't bother to pick up his cap.

Nathan and I both turned to look at Chili.

She tossed her head and flashed us a smile. "Let's not let this little spat ruin our evening, shall we, folks?"

But I knew her. And I knew that inside—behind the brave words and the confident expression—she was hurting. I was hurting a little too. Kat's nasty outburst had stolen the fun out of our evening.

NOTES TO SELF

I need to check out the Chili/Gemini love connection. Chili seems really hurt, yet she's never even had coffee with this guy. Their relationship is all in her head. Not unlike my relationship with Nathan, I guess. So I should check out myself as well. The Moon sign quiz I took this morning is a starting place. Maybe I shouldn't be so scared to feel.

MUTABLE SIGNS (GEMINI, VIRGO, SAGITTARIUS, PISCES)
WANT TO TALK ABOUT EVERYTHING. CARDINAL SIGNS
(ARIES, LIBRA, CANCER, CAPRICORN) WANT TO RUN
EVERYTHING. FIXED SIGNS (TAURUS, LEO, SCORPIO,
AQUARIUS), HOWEVER, WANT TO OWN EVERYTHING.
FREQUENTLY THOUGHT OF AS STUBBORN, THEY OFTEN
TAKE LONGER TO START, BUT ONCE THEY DO, THEY ARE
DIFFICULT TO STOP. IF YOU WANT TO BE ON A FIXED
SIGN'S GOOD SIDE, DON'T ARGUE. BE PATIENT.

—*Fearless Astrology*

he moment I realized that Frankenstein was a fixed
sign, I underlined everything I could find about him,
just as if I were preparing for one of his hideous
assignments. I didn't need an astrology book to tell me that

patience wasn't one of my greatest strengths. After his display of friendliness last night, though, I decided to step up my campaign—ever so secretly, of course. I knew his birth *day*; once I learned his time and place of birth, I could figure out the rest of his chart.

That morning Chili told us that the Gears had slashed the tires on Frankenstein's car the night before. That's what the commotion had been about. One of only three girls enrolled in auto shop, Chili had spotted his beloved restored Corvette there when she'd arrived for class. Although he brought the car to her dad's dealership for serious work, like most of the teachers, he used the school's free auto shop lab for minor repairs.

I decided to show up fifteen minutes early for English and realized too late that Dina Coulter had spotted me.

"Hi, Logan. Hi, Jared. Hi, J.T. Hi, Sol." I couldn't imagine what she and Kat talked about when they weren't at school and Dina didn't have any names to recite.

I turned into the classroom. Frankenstein was alone, and of course, he appeared to be in a foul mood. Thanks to Chili, I knew why. He loved that car and had poured a lot of money into having it restored at Chili's dad's dealership. He even put a weatherproof cover over it in the parking lot. I wasn't sure why someone willing to spend time and money restoring an old Corvette would then opt to have it painted gaudy yellow. More research and I discovered that it was a Taurus color.

"What?" he asked as I approached his desk.

He looked as if he hadn't slept, and he spoke in what my

gram would call a "whiskey tenor."

"The brownies." I handed him a folded piece of paper fresh from my printer. "You said you liked them, so I thought I'd give you the recipe."

He managed a bleary-eyed smile. "Oh, you did, did you? How'd you know I like to bake?"

"People who like food usually do." Uh-oh. The only way I could know he liked food was by what I'd read about his sign. "Besides," I gushed, "this recipe is so easy that anyone can make it. The secret is the vinegar, and the chocolate chips in the cream cheese, of course."

He gave me a doubtful look and dug into the stack of papers on his desk. "I appreciate your interest, but it's not going to buy you a grade."

"I would never . . ." I began.

"Since you're so punctual, I might as well give you this. I was here later than I planned to be last night, due to some mechanical difficulties, so I had time to finish grading them."

I looked at the numerical grade, and my heart sank. Eighty-four, barely a B. I didn't need to do the math. I was way below the average needed for the fellowship, and he wasn't going to write a glowing rec for someone who got B minuses.

"You have a problem with that?" he asked, bushy eyebrow raised.

Fixed sign, I reminded myself. *Be patient.*

"I know you're right," I said. "It's just that I tried so hard."

"Not hard enough, McRae. What is it about the *personal*

in *personal* essay that you don't understand?"

"I'm not sure." I knew I'd cry if I said another word.

"The essay is supposed to be your experience." He squinted at me, but his expression wasn't as mean as it usually was. "I wanted to know a moment that changed *your* life. I'm already acquainted with the opinions of Heraclitus and Eric Hoffer." He yanked off his glasses and stared at me from across the desk. "The only purpose of including a quote is so that you can give your interpretation of it, not to just fill space and up the word count. Get it?"

Most of the quotes had come from Paige, so I wasn't sure what to say. Class would start in a few minutes. I'd come here trying to win him over. Talk about counterproductive.

I nodded. "I guess I never thought my experiences were that important."

"Well, if you think so now, that's a major improvement," he said.

Right. But it wouldn't get me the fellowship. I'd be spending the summer here working with Chili in the office of the dealership.

"Thanks." I turned and started back to my desk.

"Saw your mom on the Golf Network," he said. "She's really on a roll, isn't she?"

"I miss her."

Oh my god, where did that come from? I never talked about her to anyone, not even my dad.

"It's got to be tough."

Sympathy from Frankenstein? I searched his face for any sign of his usual sarcasm.

"She's following her dream." That's what I always said when people questioned me about her absences.

His eyes seemed to bore through me. "And what's your dream, McRae?"

"The fellowship," I blurted. "I want to spend the summer studying writing more than I can tell you, and . . ." I looked down at the paper in my hand.

He looked at it too. "Do you think you can bring that up to snuff if I let you take another stab at it?"

"What?"

"You heard me, McRae. Now speak up before I change my mind."

"Yes," I said. "Oh, yes. I mean, thank you." Then I headed for my desk, aware that the room had filled up and everyone was watching me.

"What's going on?" Chili asked as I sat down across from her.

I just smiled. I was too happy to speak.

NOTES TO SELF

I am totally shocked that Frankenstein gave me a second chance. Maybe there is hope for the fellowship. Or was he just feeling sorry for me because I confessed that I miss my mom? She called tonight and said she'll be home soon. We don't pressure her; she has enough of that on tour. Instead, my dad and I walked around the kitchen, each of us holding a phone. "Great," he said, and I added, "Cool, Mom." Then we said good night, hung up, and hugged each other.

6

AQUARIUS. AN AIR SIGN. AQUARIANS ARE RULED BY
URANUS, THE PLANET OF ABRUPT CHANGE, AND
SATURN, THE PLANET OF REPRESSION. THE MORE
YOU DEMAND CHANGE, AQUARIUS, THE MORE YOU
NEED SECURITY. IT'S THE WORLD AROUND YOU THAT
YOU WANT TO CHANGE, AND IT WON'T.

—*Fearless Astrology*

*T*hat sounded like me, all right. I did want to change.
That's why I didn't just toss *Fearless Astrology* back
in the box. Did I also need security? I wasn't sure.
All I knew was that the two things I wanted most—the summer school fellowship and Nathan—were a lot closer than
they had been before. And it was all because of *Fearless*. I
loved what I was learning, and I wanted to use this magical
book to figure out everyone I knew.

Frankenstein had actually given me a second chance. I'd never heard of that happening, ever. Putting myself in the essay couldn't be that difficult, could it? I knew I could write, but every time I let my emotions show, my Aquarius side took over, and I analyzed my work to death.

Dad went back to work to finish a job. Chili invited us for dinner and a sleepover that night, so I made some more brownies and brought them to her mom. Stella hugged me tight and called me *honey,* which for some reason always made me feel both happy and sad.

The kitchen smelled of pilaf and some new perfume Stella had squirted around for our approval. She had just bought the line for the boutique she owned with her sister Annie, who, like her, had glossy dark hair and a fondness for what they called *bling.*

They were proud of their Armenian heritage and spent many weekends making stuffed grape leaves called *yalanchi* and layered Armenian pastries.

While we ate, Chili, Paige, and I discussed how we could get my frugal Virgo dad to finance a shopping trip for my night with Nathan. He gave me a check once a month. After that, it was my job to manage my money until the next check. I hadn't been too successful at it this March. Chili offered her Neiman card, but I didn't want to take advantage of her Gemini generosity. There had to be some way I could use my dad's sign to get what I wanted from him.

After dinner, we changed into our swimsuits and headed

barefoot across the marble floor toward the spa on the patio. The top of Chili's new black two-piece was secured by only a large chrome ring. If I tried to wear anything that daring, my dad would ground me for the rest of my life.

Paige had created her own designer knockoff bikini. Lemon yellow, it was covered in a tiny navy-and-white print that she said was taken from a Moroccan tile pattern. My blue-green tank looked as if I'd borrowed it and the body inside it from someone on the twelve-and-under swim team.

"Don't you think it's a little cold for a swim?" Stella asked Chili with that concerned expression that was as much a part of her as the spray of diamonds and gold on her ring finger.

"The spa's heated, Mom. Besides, we need to talk." At the French doors, Chili stopped briefly and added, "Privately."

"I want you back in here within the hour, honey. I mean that."

Chili ignored her and stepped out onto the deck. I followed, my bare arms and legs prickling when the cool air hit me. What could Chili want to talk about? She wasn't exactly secretive.

Once we'd pulled up our hair and settled along the curving ledge in the warm rush of bubbles, I asked, "So what's going on?"

Chili looked across the hot tub to Paige. "Tell her."

"We're doing an intervention," Paige blurted.

"What are you talking about?" I whirled around to Chili.

Her highlighted hair picked up the fiber-optic lighting that lit the water swirling around us. At the moment, it looked green with purple streaks.

"Not an intervention." She glared at Paige. "I said it was going to *be like* an intervention. All right, Logan, here's the deal. The idea was to get you somewhere where you couldn't easily escape and then force you to tell us what's going on."

As if I couldn't escape a five-foot-round spa. "I have no idea what's going on here," I said. "And I'm not sure how I feel about the two of you conspiring behind my back. We're supposed to be friends."

"We *are* friends, and we're not conspiring," Chili said. "Are we, Paige?"

"Of course not." She shook her head so vigorously that a chunk of blond hair dislodged and fell over one eye. "We just want you to tell us what's going on with you."

"Don't deny it," Chili said before I could protest. "First Nathan would barely talk to you. Now he's all cozy at school, texting you, and asking you out."

"I'm as surprised by that as you are."

"And you're suddenly, bizarrely all buddy-buddy with Frankenstein," she said.

"I was going to tell you about that." I slid down until the water was around my neck, and the pressure pushed my legs up.

"There's more," Chili said, her expression accusing. "You're different lately, Logan. It's like you've got some big secret, and you aren't sharing it with us."

"You wouldn't believe me," I told her.

"Ha. She *admits* it." Paige shot up in the water so fast that she nearly lost her top. Not that that would be so tragic. She was as flat as I was, and the only cleavage she had was built into her bikini top.

"So?" Chili demanded.

"Well, remember that big black leather book I found the other night when we were going through the closet in my house?"

"What book?" Chili asked.

"The one with the stars on the cover." Paige could hardly contain her excitement. "I knew you weren't telling us everything."

"It's about astrology." I lowered my voice. Was I really sharing this? Would they think I was a total flake?

"Go on." I could tell Chili was unconvinced. "Are you saying this book is the reason Nathan's so into you?"

"In a way. If he is, I mean." I took a deep breath. "Don't tell a soul, but I tried to do what the book said. It was about appealing to his Sun sign, and it seems to be working."

They balanced on the ledge in stunned silence for a moment. Then finally Chili spoke. "Hunh. Think it might work for me to get Trevor?"

"I already told you. You're going to get him anyway once he's over the breakup with Kat. My situation is different. I'm not gorgeous like you."

Neither of them denied that.

"Let me get this straight," Paige said slowly. "You used Nathan's Sun sign to find out how to make him like you?"

"Right."

"And what about Frankenstein?"

"You guys know I need a good recommendation from him. He's head of the fellowship committee, and he has ties at the college in Monterey."

"Are you using his Sun sign to make him like you too?" Chili asked.

I nodded. "He's a Taurus, which means sensual."

"Ew," Chili said.

"No, no, not sex. Tauruses are foodies too. I gave him some brownies, but it's going to take more than that to get what I need out of him."

I felt a flush of shame on my cheeks. Did I sound as ridiculous to them as I did to myself?

To my surprise, my friends' faces were lit with expressions I'd never seen before.

"Brilliant," Chili said to Paige. "Why didn't we think of it? Freakin' astrology."

Paige sat up, and her top slipped. "Brilliant," she repeated. "Let's put this to work."

"Me first." Chili was bouncing in the water now, splashing as she talked. "Trevor, Logan. Come on. Tell me what I can do to get him."

"Do you know his sign?" I asked.

"No, but I have his birthday in my address book."

"What about you?" Chili asked Paige. "Who do you want Logan to help you with?"

"I don't know," Paige said, her voice barely audible, as if she were holding something back.

"Well, what about . . ." Chili hoisted herself onto the built-in ledge and began to count boys off her fingers. "There's Jared Hamilton. He's cute but kind of dull. There's J.T. That might be fun, even though he's awfully tall. He and Nathan hang out with Trevor. We could all go out together."

Before we could continue, I heard a loud "*Woo*," from the bushes that lined the swimming pool. "Yo, girls," a deep male voice shouted.

Just then three guys in black ski masks—and nothing else—streaked across the backyard. I watched them disappear through Stella's sago palms, but not before I saw everything.

And I mean *everything*.

Chili shrieked and slapped her hands across her chest.

Paige sat frozen, staring at where they had been.

Stella rushed out on the patio. "Honey, was that you screaming? What's wrong?"

"The Gears of War," Chili said in a voice that tried too hard to be calm. "Guys from school, Mom. Naked. They went through the back."

NOTES TO SELF

I'm writing in my notebook in Chili's bedroom, so that I can remember exactly how it happened. I'm not sure how those boys just appeared out of nowhere. As I sit on Chili's bed staring at what I've just written, I realize what's really on my mind, and it's not the naked streaking Gears. *Fearless Astrology* isn't just my secret anymore. How do I feel about that? All right, I think. Paige and Chili don't think I'm weird. They might even be as excited about this fabulous book as I am.

WHEN OUT OF CONTROL, FIRE SIGNS CAN BE FOOL-
HARDY, EGOTISTICAL, PLAYFUL, AND CARELESS. THINK
OF FLAMES. THEY ARE BEST COMPATIBLE WITH OTHER
FLAMES, SOMETIMES EVEN WITH AIR. FIRE SIGNS MUST
AVOID EARTH SIGNS THAT SMOTHER THEM AND WATER
SIGNS THAT EXTINGUISH THEM.

—*Fearless Astrology*

The Gears were out of control. They had dashed naked across the backyard of the one high school sophomore whose father would kill them without hesitation. Older than most of the parents at the school, Chili's parents had given up on the possibility of being able to have a family until she came along, and they were beyond protective.

Stella had actually taken off in the direction Chili had

pointed. She'd then called Chili's dad, who raced home from the car dealership and, red-faced and out of breath, joined us at the Chiliderians' long dining room table.

Amazing how naked boys all looked the same when their faces were hidden. We couldn't begin to identify them, and the more Chili's parents questioned us, the more confused we got. We couldn't even prove it was the Gears, but we knew.

The phone at Chili's began to ring. The Gears hadn't stopped after leaving her place. They'd shown their naked selves all over the neighborhood, from Geneva's to Charles Bellamy's. Chili's dad took that call. He said the guy phoning was Charles's guardian, and that Charles was "deeply disturbed" by what he'd observed from his bedroom window.

Stella murmured something about "that poor boy."

Once the parents had excused us, we changed for bed. Chili wore her teal-colored monkey slippers and a tank top. Paige and I had put on our matching sleep shirts that Stella had picked up for us during one of her numerous shopping trips to "the city," which was, of course, San Francisco.

Chili and I stretched out on our stomachs on the pink comforter that covered the bed. She'd already turned up the new Alicia Keys CD in case Stella was still in protective mode and eavesdropping outside the door.

"They'll probably post pictures of us all over school," she moaned.

"You, maybe," I said. "I don't know why they'd bother with me, but I didn't see any flashes, and I think they were moving too fast to take photos anyway."

Paige sat across from us in front of the cherry wood armoire where Chili's computer lived. Her long blond hair, which had gotten soaked during the Gears' invasion, was pulled straight back from her face. Without her glasses and in spite of her pale lashes, her eyes looked enormous.

"Do you think you could help identify them, Logan?"

"How?" I asked. "I didn't see them any longer than you did."

Then I realized Paige had that awestruck expression on her face again. "*You* know," she said.

"Of course! By their Sun signs." Chili jumped from the bed. "Can you figure out what sign someone would have to be to be a member of the Gears?"

"Maybe." Could I really find out something like that with my limited knowledge?

"What do you mean *maybe*?" Chili asked. "What does the book say?"

She and Paige both seemed to be holding their breaths, waiting for my brilliant response. Only problem was I didn't have one.

"Aries, Leo, Sagittarius are fire signs." I sat up on the bed. "You're an air sign, Chili." Oh, was she ever. I nodded toward Paige. "The Fish over there is water."

Paige wrung out her ponytail. "Well, at least I look the part."

"So the Gears are what?" Chili asked.

"Fire signs, I'd say. Not for sure. I just mean a fire sign might do something like this, but so would a lot of signs, especially those with fire in their charts."

"You mean you can have fire and not *be* fire?" Chili asked.

"That's right." I turned to her and asked what I'd been wondering since we started this conversation. "Hey, Chili, why is it so important for me to figure out who the Gears are?"

"They invaded my backyard," she said. "Naked."

"Shocking." Paige made no attempt to hide the amusement in her voice.

"Naked boys," I added, and made a creepy face at her. "Kind of fun, wasn't it?"

"Maybe," Chili conceded, "but what they wrote about Ms. Snider was pretty rotten. You agree with that, don't you?"

"Of course, but why do we care who they are?"

"Because it's important. If we identify the Gears, do you realize how cool we'll be?"

"Cool so that you can get Trevor?" I should have seen that one coming. "How many times have I told you that you're going to get him anyway?"

"Based on recent events in a certain school parking lot, I find that pretty doubtful." It was indifferent Chili again, and I knew what she was trying to cover with it.

"You have his birth date in your address book, right?"

"Let me get it." She stood up and opened the armoire to a Gemini clutter of paper, index cards, and sticky notes. A couple of mouse swipes, and she had it. "November one," she said, then got up and flopped down on the bed. "Tell me everything."

"Scorpio." I'd already memorized the dates for Sun signs.

"What does that mean? Is it good?"

"Intense and emotional," I said. "Secretive too. Doesn't sound much like Trevor, does it? Isn't he kind of just your basic jock?"

"Basic *hot* jock." Chili glanced at Paige. "What do you think?"

Paige drew her knees up under her nightshirt, only the tips of her toes peeking out. "Well, last night with Kat sounded pretty intense and emotional, wouldn't you say?"

"And maybe he is secretive," I said. "I mean, he's supposed to be split from Kat, yet she obviously doesn't think so."

"I don't like secrets." Chili clasped her hands together and rested her chin on them. "But I like him."

"It wouldn't be a bad match," I said. "There have been some famous Scorpio and Gemini couples in history."

"Oh, tell us," Paige said.

"I'd need the book for that and I left it at home."

"Well, let's go get it." Chili was already off the bed, digging in her closet for something to throw over her very short tank top and boy shorts.

"Are you sure?" I asked. "You know if we get caught, your parents will kill us."

"If the Gears can run naked through my backyard, we can drive down the street to get a book." She tossed me a long sweater. "The garage is on this side of the house. They won't even know we're gone."

"Except for Stella, who's probably crouched outside your

bedroom door," Paige said.

"That's where you come in." Chili grinned. "If she is around, just tell her we're in the bathroom, washing our hair, and we can't come out just yet. Mom understands hair."

"I can handle that." Paige seemed relieved that she didn't have to accompany us on our wild ride to my house.

"That might work," I said.

"Of course it will." Chili clicked open the lock on her sliding glass door that led to the side yard, that led to the garage, that led to the book, that led to who knew what?

I followed her. The sweater didn't provide much protection from the cold.

"It smells like rain," I told Chili.

"We'll get back before it starts."

Miraculously, we managed to get out of the tandem garage and the driveway with no problem. Chili glanced at me from the corner of her eye.

"Once you figure out the Gears, Frankenstein will realize how brilliant you are. You know that, don't you?"

I hadn't thought about that. Maybe I could use *Fearless* to help me find them. Maybe that would win Frankenstein's approval.

"You've convinced me," I told her as we turned onto my street. "There's got to be a way to identify the Gears by their signs, and I'm going to try to do it."

"I know you can," she said. "Here we are. Let's go get that book."

My dad wasn't home yet. The lonely feel of our house hit me in the chest.

Chili tapped my arm. "You all right?"

"Just have to find my backpack." Why was I whispering? No one was home. No one was ever home.

I headed down the tiled hall to my bedroom. No backpack.

"I thought I left it on the bed," I said. Then I spotted it on my dresser. "There it is."

"At last." Chili grabbed it and rummaged through my lip gloss and breath mints. She looked from it to me and said, "There's no astrology book in here."

"That's crazy. Of course there is." It was always in my backpack.

I grabbed it and started digging. Nothing. No book. I began to panic.

"It's all right." Chili squeezed my shoulder. "You probably just forgot where you put it."

"I know exactly where I put it. Someone took it." A little shiver ran through me. I tried to ignore it.

"Well, even if you lost it, there are lots of other ones out there, right?"

"No, they won't be *this* one. It won't be the same."

"All right," she said. "Let's backtrack. Where was the book the last time you saw it?"

"In my backpack."

"And where was the backpack?"

I realized how dependent I'd become on the book. "On my bed."

"Who has access to your bedroom?"

"No one. My dad never touches my stuff."

"Maybe he borrowed it."

"For what?"

We went into his room anyway. Beside his desk, shoved in a steel-mesh wastebasket, I saw it, not even hidden, sitting right on top.

All I could say was "Why?"

"At least we found it," Chili said.

"Yes." I hugged it to me. But I kept asking myself that same question. *Why?*

NOTES TO SELF

I totally panicked when we thought the book was gone. I can't explain how relieved I am to have it back. I've got to find out why my dad took it without even asking. And I will just as soon as he gets home tonight. I realize now that he and I have been living on a teeter-totter. We're polite and kind to each other, and we say only good things about Mom. It's as if we know that if one of us moves too fast or gets angry and jumps off, the teeter-totter will come crashing down, and someone will get hurt. Tonight, though, we are going to have to talk. Really talk.

8

VIRGO IS THE NITPICKY PARENT OF THE UNIVERSE.
RUN THE OTHER WAY IF YOU CAN. IF YOU CAN'T RUN,
IF YOU LOVE A VIRGO AND ARE WORRIED BY THE COM-
PULSIVE DEMANDS THIS PERSON INFLICTS ON YOUR
LIFE, DON'T GIVE UP. WANT SOMETHING FROM A
VIRGO? PRETEND TO CONSIDER ALL THE VERBOSE
LOGIC. THEN, VERY QUIETLY, NEGOTIATE.

—*Fearless Astrology*

Virgo. Sign of Blake Lively, Beyoncé, and my dad.

I sent Chili back home.

"But you told me you'd help with Trevor," she said.

"I promise I'll do it tomorrow. I'm sorry, but I just can't right now."

She nodded, and I knew she understood that I was serious

about needing to be alone.

In a kitchen cabinet, I found a box of chai tea my mom had bought the last time she was home. In less than an hour, I heard the garage door open. By then, I was on my third cup. There are some things in the world that taste better as you consume more of them. Let me say that chai tea isn't one.

Because the kitchen table was too big for us now, my dad and I usually ate at the white-tiled counter in front of the stove. That's where I was when he walked in.

His face usually lit up when he saw me. Tonight, his expression was guarded.

"Hey, I thought you were staying at Chili's."

Raindrops beaded on his tan jacket. His red-brown hair was damp and slightly curly, starting to frizz.

"I was." I lifted the book from the counter. "But I decided to come back for this."

He didn't even bother pretending.

"I don't want you reading that stuff, Logan. It will bring you nothing but trouble."

"Couldn't you have discussed it with me before you took my property?"

"It's not your property." He stopped himself, then said, "You're right, though. I should have told you instead of just taking it."

"Told me what, Dad?"

He ran his fingers through his hair and headed for the refrigerator. Then he started laying out his omelet ingredients neatly along the tiles. I waited until he faced me across the counter. Realizing that I wasn't going away or allowing him to change the subject, he said, "I don't want you messing around with astrology at your age. It's not good for you."

"Why don't you let me decide that?"

"I should have." He cracked and whisked eggs in a clear glass bowl as if grateful for an excuse to avoid meeting my eyes. "I was running late when I saw that you had the book. And I didn't—I didn't think it through, I guess."

The beaten eggs hissed into the sizzling butter. Smells of comfort filled the room.

"Whose book is it?" I asked. "Not Mom's?"

"Of course not." He reached for the spatula and tilted the pan, lifting the corners of the yellow mixture. Then he gave me that clear-eyed, serious expression I'd always trusted. "Tell you what. I'll apologize for not talking it over with you, if you'll agree to put the book back where you found it, all right?"

Which meant that he would win. All he had to do was apologize. But I'd have to give up the book. Just then, I remembered what Chili had said earlier. *There are lots of astrology books out there.*

I glanced over at it beside me on the counter. "So you hate every astrology book, or just this one?"

That seemed to take him by surprise. His expression became even more guarded.

"We're talking about *this* book, Logan."

Typical Virgo logic. Avoiding my question with another

statement.

"*This* book," I said. "Where did it come from, and why does it matter if I want to keep it?"

"You have free will, honey." He tapped his finger on the top of the counter. "Free." - *Tap.* "Will."- *Tap.* "But I love you, and I don't want your life limited because of something you read in a book about how you're supposed to be or not be."

"Your astrological chart is a suggestion, not a life sentence," I quoted from the foreword. "Understanding tendencies only makes us aware. If you had a tendency to drive fast, wouldn't an awareness of the possible consequences of that benefit you?"

"Stop," he said. "You don't even sound like yourself."

"And you don't sound like yourself either, Dad. Remember what you always told me about censorship? That I should be free to read whatever I choose?"

This was probably not the time to mention the copy of the *Kama Sutra* Chili, Paige, and I *borrowed* from Paige's folks' beach cabin last summer.

"You are free to read whatever." He bit his lip, as if trying to hold back words he'd regret. "I'm just strongly suggesting that you spend your time on something more productive than astrology. Mr. Franklin's class, for instance."

Ouch. Where had that come from? All he'd said before now was that he knew I had what it took to get the fellowship.

"Actually, I have been working with Mr. Franklin," I said. Good thing he didn't know I'd been doing it with astrology and cream cheese brownies.

Dad picked up the spatula and cut the omelet in two perfect pieces, not a single morsel out of place. That gave me an idea, one straight from the book: *Then, very quietly, negotiate.*

"Pure Virgo," I said.

His face flushed. "What are you talking about?"

"Just that Virgos like order and control. The way you have to run across a room to straighten any picture that isn't properly aligned."

"That's ridiculous. Everyone does that."

"Maybe," I said. "You're your own person and can break any stereotype, can't you?"

"Of course."

"Especially the thrifty wrap."

"What are you getting at?"

"Dad, I'm going out tomorrow night, and I really need something cool to wear."

The spoonful of salsa he was arranging around our plates splattered on the counter. "Clothes come out of *your* budget," he said. "Remember?"

"Spoken like a true Virgo." I forced myself to meet his eyes.

"Logan." He gave me a sad smile. "I know it's tough on you this year with Mom gone so much, but don't go looking for magic solutions, all right?"

"Astrology isn't magic," I said.

"That's not my point." He sighed. "If I advance you some money for clothes, will you put the book away?"

Now, that was tempting. I glanced down at it, those tarnished little silver stars and the secrets they held.

"I wouldn't ask you to give up something that made you happy."

"And the book does that?"

I nodded. "It makes me feel . . . I don't know."

He put the plate in front of me. "Just don't take what you read there as pure fact, will you?" Then he reached in his pocket for his wallet. "Now, eat your eggs."

NOTES TO SELF

Dad comes through for me even when he tries not to. I'm keeping the book *and* getting a clothes contribution. I'm so lucky to have him, especially when Mom's on tour. Can't wait for tomorrow to go shopping with Paige and Chili. But am I maybe *too* into this book?

9

Ruled by Venus, Libra can be one of the beauties of the zodiac. So why is this sign so clingy? For those who don't mind a constant hand on a shoulder, an arm, or wherever, a Libra can offer a sense of security. Until the criticism kicks in—and it always does. The way to understand a Libra is to remind yourself that this person moves through life looking in the mirror. The focus will never be on you. If you can live with that, you'll be just fine.

—Fearless Astrology

closed the book and pressed the cover against me. Then, I put it back in my backpack. Paige and Chili had been shocked and happy that my dad had financed my little shopping spree. With their help, after school, I bought a sweater and some new straight-leg jeans that, once Paige made some alterations, wouldn't be too clunky when I tried to walk or climb into a certain Honda. Which I'd be climbing into very soon, thank you very much. They'd even talked me into a beret the color of charcoal. Loving my clothes but hating my frizzy hair, I'd pulled out a chunk and given myself instant bangs with a pair of scissors Paige had used when she hemmed my jeans. They both shrieked but admitted I looked better.

All I could think about was what I'd be doing tonight, and who I'd be doing it with. I put everything but the Frankenstein essay on hold and read all I could about Nathan. According to the chart in the back, his Moon was in Libra.

The Moon stuff was starting to make sense to me now. With only the date and year of birth, I could find anyone's Moon on the chart at the back of *Fearless Astrology*. Once I had that, I could figure out the influences on the Sun sign. A strong moon such as Aries would create a fiery influence on a Sun sign. That could be good for a dreamy Pisces like Paige and not so good for someone like Nathan, who already had plenty of fire in his Sun sign.

Instead of fire, his Moon was air, and pretty cold indeed. Nathan wasn't, though. He was always going out of his way to help people in need, like shaving off his hair for the Kids and Cancer benefit, although he looked even hotter with his head shaved. Could he know that? Didn't matter. Tonight was the night and, yes, I was so nervous that I could barely keep my teeth from chattering.

"Nervous?" Chili asked as we drove to school that morning.

"Gee, how can you tell?"

Paige giggled from the backseat. "Well, don't be," she said. "The bangs are perfect. No more mad-scientist hair."

I turned around to face her. "What you did with those jeans—I can't believe it."

"I used one pin on each leg," she said. "That's all you need for a simple job like that."

"You're going to be a fabulous designer," I told her, and started to get nervous again. "I hope Nathan likes them as much as I do."

"Nathan likes *you*." Chili grinned as we drove into the school parking lot. "Whatever you did with that book worked *and* will keep working. Now, let's figure out how to get Trevor for me."

"Absolutely," I said. "I can tell by the way he looks at you that that is going to be way easier than trying to figure out the Gears."

Frankenstein was relatively nice to me in class that day, meaning that he didn't demand that I participate or ask any questions about my mom. I pulled my sweater tight against the freezing wind and hurried toward auto shop to meet

Chili. All of a sudden, there I was, face-to-face with Geneva. Well, more like face-to-chest, as if I needed a reminder.

"Hey, Logan," Geneva said in that slow-paced way of hers. "Like your bangs."

"Thanks."

"Um, got a minute?"

"Sure. I have to meet Chili, but no problem."

What else was I going to say? That it was cold out here, and I didn't want to stand there freezing my butt off when I could be in a warm building?

She didn't seem to notice the weather. Her puffy lavender jacket wasn't even zipped.

Shoving her hands into the pockets of her jeans, she said, "I understand you want to start an astrology column that focuses on teachers."

"I mentioned it to Ms. Snider, yeah. Lots of school newspapers have them."

"Um." Her amused smile was accompanied by raised brows over those almond-shaped blue-gray eyes. "And you're going to start out by trashing Frankenstein, right?"

"Not at all." How had she gotten that idea? "I just wanted to write the first one about him because—" I tried to think of a way to explain why I'd been studying his sign.

Geneva didn't seem to notice that I was scrambling for words. "That's a little disappointing. Other papers trash teachers, you know."

Not teachers who hold kids' futures in their hands. And

certainly not teachers who have given one certain kid a second chance at a personal essay.

"Writing about astrology is better than slamming him or anyone else."

"Astrology, huh?"

She might as well have said *cafeteria spinach*.

"Yeah. The teacher profile would be the minor part of the column. The rest would be about each teacher's sign, which would be the same sign as any number of kids. Who wouldn't want to learn what their strengths and weaknesses are? Not to mention . . ." I paused for emphasis, " . . . their romantic compatibilities."

"Boy/girl stuff? I take it that means you believe some signs are more compatible than others."

"They are." I dug for the most bizarre famous couples fact in the book and couldn't remember a single one.

"Well?" She shoved her hands deeper into her lavender pockets.

"It's true," I said. "Take Mr. Franklin, a fixed earth sign. He's not going to get along with a fast-talking, frequently superficial air sign like Gemini. He might be better suited for another earth sign." *Like Capricorn. Like Snider.*

"How do you know Frankenstein is earth?" That look of superiority seemed as natural to her as her rich voice.

"I believe that's the case."

Believe, right. As if I hadn't run a whole yellow highlighter out of ink on the Taurus section of the book.

"So?" Geneva crossed her arms and peered down at me.

"So I'm excited about the possibility of a column that combines teacher interviews with astrology."

"Interesting." Geneva rubbed her hands over the sleeves of her jacket. "Now tell me why we're freezing our butts off out here when we could be talking inside a warm building."

Why did it sound so much better when she said what I'd been thinking all along?

"I was wondering the same thing," I replied, and headed toward auto shop.

Geneva stepped inside the shop lab and wrinkled her nose as if offended by the motor oil or whatever it was in the air.

"Chili must hate this place," she said. "Whatever it takes, though, if she expects to take over Daddy's car dealership someday, right?"

"Chili loves auto shop, actually." I stopped short of reminding her that Chili and Charles Bellamy were the top two students in shop. Instead, I said, "Geminis are attracted to gathering information. That's part of her sign too."

"So what do you think *my* sign is?" Geneva stopped in the hall and posed before me, hand on her hip.

No denying she was gorgeous. And a limelight hog. Could be Libra. Maybe Leo. As snarky as she'd been about Chili's interest in auto shop, she could even be a gossipy Aries.

"I'd need your birth date, time, and place," I said.

"No problem. In fact, I think it's an excellent idea. A columnist for any newspaper should have to try out, don't you think?"

"I've been writing for *The Growl* since last year when I was a freshman." I hated the way my voice trembled.

"But only, um, well, just features, right?"

"An astrology column *is* a feature, Geneva."

Where was Chili? I needed to get away from this girl before I told her what I really thought.

"And you realize that before I can just hand you a column, you need to prove yourself in some way, don't you?"

"So what do you want from me?"

"An audition." She took a piece of notepaper out of her jacket pocket. "Here are two birth dates. Let me know what you figure out about them, especially compatibility."

She'd written them down before she'd even spoken to me today. How conniving was that?

I looked down at the notepaper. The first date listed was pure Libra. Guess who?

The second was Leo. And not just any Leo. Nathan's birth date was on that paper in my hand.

"Well?" Geneva asked.

Before I could wonder how much of what I felt was plastered on my face, I saw Chili coming down the hall straight for me.

"I'll get back to you," I said, and ran to Chili. If anyone could figure out what to do next, my Gemini friend would.

NOTES TO SELF

The Star Crossed column started as only an excuse to trick Frankenstein into telling me his birthday. Now it can actually happen. If it does, I can prove to him that I'm a real writer worthy of his recommendation. Geneva is my ticket. But now, in order to get the assignment, I'll have to actually figure out how astrologically simpatico she and Nathan are. If I jump off the roof tonight, you'll understand why. Good thing I live in a single-story house.

IO

LEO WANTS AN AUDIENCE, NOT A CRITIC. APPLAUD
AND ASK QUESTIONS. MOST OF ALL, REMEMBER, LEO IS
KING OF THE ZODIAC, AND IT'S ALL ABOUT THE LION,
NOT ABOUT THE OTHER PEOPLE IN HIS LIFE. IF YOU'RE
AT A LOSS FOR WORDS WITH A LEO, TRY THAT SIMPLE
THREE-LETTER WORD, Y-O-U. WORKS EVERY TIME.

—*Fearless Astrology*

eo. Sign of Hayden Panettiere, Elijah Kelley, and
Joe Jonas. The more I read about Leo, the more I
realized how perfect Nathan was for me.

"Geneva wants you to figure out
how compatible she and Nathan are?" Chili waved away the
thought as we left auto shop. "Logan, she's using you."

"I get that." How good it felt to talk to a semisane person
again.

"I wouldn't do her one favor," she said. "You're the one who's going out with him tonight. Just see what happens. Then decide."

"You're right." I stopped and realized the importance of what she'd just said. "Tonight. Oh my god."

"You'll be fabulous." She grabbed my arm and squeezed it.

"I'll try to be," I said.

"You will be." Her dark eyes flashed. "Just remember you have the "book.""

I tried to remember that when I saw the Civic hybrid's headlights splash onto the driveway that night. I tried to remember Chili's words when I heard the doorbell ring.

"I'll get it," my dad called out.

Just my luck that he had gotten off early for a change.

"No, I can—" I ran from the window to the front door, but Dad was already there, pumping Nathan's hand.

"So good to see you again."

Nathan gave him a confused smile, then said, "Oh, right. My father's your attorney, isn't he?"

"He sure is." My dad was all charm, trying way too hard to be cool. "Great people. Wish we saw more of your mom, though. Tell them I said hi. Can I get you a coffee?"

Even though he'd lived in California most of his life, he'd had never gotten it through his head that, out here, unlike

Pennsylvania, it was *a cup* of coffee.

Nathan looked vaguely horrified. "Thanks, but we're going to get some, I mean, one."

"Well, have a great night."

"Dad," I said in a soft but firm voice that clearly communicated *butt out*.

He backed away from the door. "Hi, honey. Just chatting with Nat here."

"*Nathan*," I corrected, and shot him my darkest look. "See you later."

"Finally." Nathan watched as I closed the front door behind me. Then he said, "Wow."

When I saw the expression on his face, it was all I could do to stay calm. He liked what he saw. There was no mistaking that. Thank you, Chili and Paige. Now I just needed to use my new astrology skills to make sure he stayed as dazed as he appeared to be. Being a Leo, he wouldn't be entirely focused on me for long. He'd be needing some attention.

"Sorry about my dad," I said. "I'm the only kid, and he's a little too interested in my life."

Nathan grinned. "As Frankenstein would say, 'That's the understatement of the year.'"

"And as Frankenstein would also say . . ." I gave him a lame thumbs-up. "'Ditto.'"

Once we were in the Honda, he leaned over and seemed to just stare at me. I felt myself squirm.

"What?" I asked.

"Your eyes. They're beautiful." He moved closer, then seemed to stop himself.

I sat there, my lips parted for the kiss that didn't happen. For some reason, I remembered my gram's line about catching flies if you held your mouth open and I had to stifle a giggle.

"What is it?" he asked. "What's so funny?"

"Nothing," I said, and knew I'd broken the mood. I needed to think fast.

"You're the one with the wonderful eyes, Nathan."

"Me?" His grin was immediate, and I knew the book was right again.

"They're like liquid turquoise."

"Thanks." He was glowing now, so cute I couldn't believe I was in the same vehicle, the same world as him. "On that happy note, let's get out of here before your dad changes his mind."

"Where are we going?" I asked him.

He started down the block and smiled back at me. "I'm still thinking about that."

"Meaning?"

"Meaning I'd planned to take you to the drama classroom to help us build sets." He gave me a sly smile. "Right now, though, I'm thinking we should just go somewhere and talk. Would that be all right?"

Absolutely. But that wasn't what would work with this Leo. I needed to bring it back to him, and fast.

"I'd love to help you build sets." I did my best to sound sincere.

"You sure?"

I nodded. "Since you're going to be the lead in the play, I think it's a good idea to pitch in and help, isn't it?"

He chuckled. "Frankenstein hasn't made it official yet, but everyone is sure I've got it."

"I told you that."

"And I want to believe you're right."

"You should."

I looked up at him. Other than that time back in junior high when Geneva's younger brother, Jared, and I had sneaked outside in the middle of an open house, this was the first time I'd been alone with a boy I liked. I was as speechless now as I was then.

"And you're honestly willing to work on sets?" Nathan asked. "To tell you the truth, we're really behind."

"Sure." I looked up into his eyes. "We can talk later. Right now, you need to show your support for the drama department."

This was better than I could have hoped for.

The minute we pulled into the parking lot, I spotted the cover that I knew protected Frankenstein's immaculate yellow Corvette.

"Oh, no," Nathan said. "Frankenstein."

"He's not so bad."

The temptation to explain how he could win over that Taurus Sun sign was on my lips, but I didn't dare go there.

Dina Coulter was the first one who spotted us. Her dark hair was pulled back, and she was covered by a paint spattered smock.

"Hi, Nathan. Hi, Logan."

The auditorium smelled like a nail salon. Pieces of stage sets were scattered everywhere. I was surprised to see both Trevor and Kat lifting their brushes to Frankenstein's loud directions. Kat looked fabulous in a belted jacket that skimmed her curvy shape. How could she work in something that close-fitting? Neither she nor Trevor looked at each other, and they were at least ten feet apart. Still, if Chili really wanted Trevor, and I knew she did, good old *Fearless Astrology* had better offer up a little background on Kat's sign as well as his.

"Hiiii, Logan," Kat gushed.

What was that all about? I looked at her, absolutely speechless. Why was a senior snotty cheerleader type even acknowledging a lowly sophomore?

"Hi," I said, and because I didn't have a clue what to say next, I muttered, "Nice jacket."

"Thanks." She said it so fast that it sounded like *Thinks*, something I doubted she did a lot of.

Ms. Snider was there too, pulling furniture around on the stage. She wore a black top and gray pants, and I wondered if she was trying to dress even more conservatively after what the Gears had said about her.

I hammered nails, got paint on my new jeans, and didn't care. All night long we laughed and talked. About Nathan, of course, but that was the plan.

"My mom's kind of distant." Hammer, hammer. "She's had

some problems . . ." Hammer ". . . since my dad got so successful . . ." Hammer ". . . and since my brother got sick."

"I didn't know your brother was sick." I said it quietly, so
that if he didn't want to respond, he could pretend he hadn't
heard it.

"He's doing pretty well now." He looked up and met my
eyes. "It's tough, though. That's why I get involved in this
stuff." He gestured toward his shaved head. "I've never told
this to anyone, Logan."

Because I didn't know what else to say, I touched his arm
and said, "I'm glad you told me."

A big glob of purple paint splashed on my hand.

"Oh, no." Nathan put down his brush, grabbed a rag, and
began to rub it off. He glanced into my eyes and smiled.

I looked down at him and knew I was smiling, too.

When he drove me home, he parked at the farthest end of
the circular drive. Not good enough. The place exploded into
lights. Good old Dad. Nathan pulled away from me as fast as
I did from him.

"Well," he said, "so much for the kiss I had in mind."

I leaned close to him. "Doesn't bother me if it doesn't
bother you."

He lowered his head, then covered my lips with his, softly
at first. He smelled of soap and tasted like coffee. My head
began to spin. I couldn't believe it. That first kiss after the
dance—the one I'd hung every hope on—couldn't begin to
compare with this.

"Your dad will be out here any minute." His voice was husky, his lips wet against my cheek.

I turned, breathed in his warm breath, and said, "You're probably right."

His fingers tangled in my hair as if ready to pull me to him once more. So much for the hat.

"Promise me you'll see me again."

"Of course. I need to go inside now."

"Yeah, I know you have to, but . . ." His expression was almost enough to make me forget about my dad.

But not quite.

Especially not with him strolling out of the house, hairy legs and all, in the emerald green velour bathrobe my mom bought for him two Christmases ago. Poor Dad. If I weren't so annoyed, I might have felt sorry for him.

"Evening," he said. "Just taking out the trash."

With that, he went over to the side yard and began dragging the garbage cans to the curb. No need to mention to Nathan that the garbage was picked up on Mondays. I was embarrassed enough already.

"Thanks for tonight," I told him. "I'd better get inside now, or he'll start mowing the lawn."

"I meant what I said." His eyes were shadowed in the dim light. He picked up the hat from my lap and pulled it down almost over my eyes. "I want to get together again, Logan. Really soon."

I peered up from the darkness and said, "Me too."

NOTES TO SELF

Nathan likes me. Whatever the book told me to do must have worked. I'll get another night with him, another chance to kiss him. Can't wait! The fellowship is still a possibility, and life is soon going to be perfect. So why am I so anxious? In a word, Geneva. Might as well check out *Fearless Astrology* and confront the facts before I go to bed. Who knows? Maybe Nathan and Geneva are the worst-suited couple since Brad and Jen. Let's hope.

LEO AND LIBRA CAN BE AN EXCELLENT MATCH AS LONG AS THEY LOVE EACH OTHER ENOUGH TO SHARE CENTER STAGE. BOTH ARE ATTRACTIVE PERSONALITIES; BOTH LOVE ATTENTION. LEO'S FIXED FIRE, AND LIBRA IS CARDINAL AIR. THEY WILL HAVE EITHER HOT, PASSIONATE LOVE OR HOT, PASSIONATE FIGHTS. BOTH ARE TAKE-CHARGE TYPES. LEO JUMPS IN AND JUST DOES IT. LIBRA MANIPULATES. IF THEY DON'T CONFLICT OVER WHO GETS THE ATTENTION, THESE TWO CAN ENJOY A LONG-LASTING RELATIONSHIP.

—*Fearless Astrology*

*L*ibra. Sign of Zac Efron, Ashlee Simpson, and Hillary Duff. As if Geneva wasn't sexy enough. To make it worse, I discovered that she had a Leo Moon. I rechecked just to be sure. Afraid so. She was a Libra with a Leo Moon, and Nathan was a Leo with a Libra Moon. Opposite sides of the same coin. What was I going to do?

"What are you going to do?" Chili echoed my thoughts. She was getting her highlights done that Saturday, and Paige and I sat with her in the salon waiting for the color to cook into her hair. She patted at the foil packets on her head. "You could lie."

"Can't," I said.

All right, I'll admit it. That was my first thought too. I mean, would anyone with a shred of sanity announce the fact that the guy she wanted—the guy whose kiss she could still taste—and the hottest girl in school were perfect astrological soul mates? No! I should tell her that Leo and Libra were the worst combination on the planet.

"Agreed." Paige looked up from the magazine she was flipping through. "You'd get caught."

"How?" Chili demanded.

"Because any astrology book could prove me wrong. I'd come out looking pathetic, stupid, or both."

"You really think Geneva would go to the trouble of checking?" Chili met my eyes in the mirror.

"She might if she wants Nathan enough."

"So you have to tell her?" Paige looked up from her magazine again.

"Only if she asks," I said.

I reminded myself that I didn't know enough about the influence of the other planets in Geneva's and Nathan's charts. Beside, as the book said, *the Sun sign is not the sum.* I'd need to make that clear to Geneva. If I talked to her at all. If I told her anything.

I'd been planning to catch up with her on Monday in journalism class. But have I mentioned that my life doesn't always work out according to plan? Chili had lost her car keys, and once her highlights were as perfect as always, we had to get a copy of the keys made. Afterward, we walked around the mall and looked for shoes for Chili to buy for *Operation Trevor,* as she now called it. Scorpios were big on style, I'd told her, although you'd never guess that from looking at Trevor's jock attire.

"What I need . . . " She turned around in front of the mirror in our favorite shop and lifted the sandals she was trying on. "What I really need is a pair of combat boots to kick Kat's ass right out of Trevor's life."

Paige giggled.

"What you need is a gemstone that corresponds to your Sun sign," I told her. "Amethyst, I think the book says."

Their faces lit up again. And, yes, I was starting to like this, well, *power.* Maybe I had some Leo in *my* sign.

"Let's go." Chili kicked off the sandals. "Where do you buy

an amethyst in this town?"

"Let me check the book first to be sure that's the right stone," I said.

We were on our way out of the store when we nearly ran into Geneva. The breeze tossed her cropped hair across her face. She shoved it back and still looked great.

"Well, look who's here." She glanced down at us with an amused expression that must have passed for friendly in her mind. Then her gaze settled on me. "Cool top, Logan."

My face must have been the same shade as the red patent belt Paige had talked me into wearing with the black-and-white rugby tee.

"Thanks," I said.

"Very few people can wear horizontal stripes." Before I could recover from the Libra backhand, she added, "I've been thinking about you."

Chili and Paige whirled their heads so quickly toward me that I was afraid they'd get whiplash.

"You have?"

The wind was blowing my own hair. I wished I had my fabulous new beret, and I remembered for a moment how it felt when Nathan pulled it down over my eyes as we sat in my driveway.

"Yep. I was wondering what you found out about the sign of Libra."

I paused. Looked at Paige, at Chili, then back at this girl who could give me the newspaper column with a snap of those long, tapered fingers. I had to show her that I knew something about astrology.

"Libras can be beautiful," I said, "but then, you probably don't need me to tell you that."

Although her laugh was low-pitched and sophisticated as always, a pink tinge spread over her cheeks. "Hunh, what else?"

Chili and Paige stood mute as statues.

"Libras tend to be fair," I said, and hoped it was the truth. "They hold the scales of justice and can sometimes be a little wishy-washy, even envious."

"Oh?"

"But only because they're trying so hard to be balanced and to see both sides of an issue."

"What about the other birth date I gave you?" She tilted her head.

"Leo." My voice scratched out the word.

"And?" she urged.

Why lie? I'd be caught anyway.

"A very *auspicious* match," I said, using the book's term, then quickly added because I just couldn't help it, "Of course, the Sun sign is not the sum. There are other factors. Moon sign, Mars, Venus. All possible to check, of course."

"Logan, I so absolutely want you to do the Star Crossed column for the paper." Although her voice was still low, it was more intense now. Her expression wasn't all that different from the way Chili and Paige had looked at me that night in the spa when I told them about the book. "Where did you learn all this?"

"Here and there."

"She's amazing," Chili blurted. "You wouldn't believe all she can do with it."

"Like what?"

I tried to jerk a silent *no* with my head. Chili caught it, but that wasn't going to do me any good. Paige was the one Geneva was nailing with that lie-detector look of hers.

"Lots of things." Paige licked her lips. "Logan's going to ID the Gears."

"She is?" Geneva turned wide eyes on me. "You are?"

"No," I said.

"Yes," Chili shouted. "She's brilliant with this stuff, Geneva. If anyone can find out who the Gears are, Logan can."

Geneva stepped back. Articulate Geneva. Perfect Geneva. Never-without-a-quick-comeback Geneva. Her gaze darted from Chili to Paige and finally rested on me. Slowly her lips curved into that infamous grin.

"No shit?" she said.

NOTES TO SELF

So now I have to find out who the Gears are through their birth signs. As luck would have it, I'll be trying to do it while Mercury is in retrograde. More on that problematic little phenomenon in a minute. I'm starting to understand the *fearless* in *Fearless Astrology*. Still, I remember what my life was like before I found the book—how I stumbled over my tongue when I tried to talk to Frankenstein, how miserable I felt when I saw Nathan and Geneva together in the parking lot. No way would I go back. Plus, I got the column. And that puts me closer to Frankenstein, and closer to the fellowship.

It just flashed into my head that running into Geneva today was no accident. There's only one reason she'd lower herself to stalk me. She thinks I know my astro stuff. Let's hope she's right.

Many fear Mercury in retrograde, and much can go wrong, but in truth, it simply slows one down, and sometimes it's good to slow down. Mercury, which is only visible before sunrise or just after sunset, travels in a forward direction most of the time. Three, maybe four times a year, it appears to travel backward for approximately three weeks. An optical illusion, of course, it does cause minor havoc, especially in communications. It can be a time of lost car keys and broken electrical equipment, and is considered an inopportune time to sign contracts or begin new projects. Instead of fighting the natural flow, use this quiet time to recheck, recharge, reflect.

—Fearless Astrology

h, yes, Mercury was in retrograde, all right. Chili was dealing with more than lost keys. The stylist who'd highlighted her hair must have left some of the bleach on. After we left the shop, Paige noticed that the streaks were turning orange. Then they began to look like the Yield signs along the sides of the freeway ramps. Not exactly a complement to her cute sapphire blue tee and gray jumper.

We marched right back to the salon. The stylist's Botoxed forehead practically exploded with worried frown lines when she saw Chili.

"There's got to be something wrong with this batch of color," she told her. "Come back in two hours, and I'll redo it, no charge, and please tell your mom I'm so sorry. I don't know what's going on."

I knew what was going on, of course, and so did Chili and Paige.

"Freakin' retrograde," Chili said once we were outside the shop again.

I couldn't help smiling. Chili—such a Gemini—was already tossing around terminology that none of us would have known a week ago.

"Hits you harder because of your sign, and because Mercury's your ruling house," I said. "You'll be all right, though."

"Easy for you to say." Chili clicked open the door locks on the Spyder.

"Wait a minute," I said. "I'm stressing too, now that Geneva knows I'm trying to figure out who the Gears are."

"We're just trying to help." Paige put a hand on my shoulder. Her butter-yellow skirt matched her hair. She looked the way she did when we were in junior high, and she was the self-appointed peacemaker.

"I know."

"You wanted the column, didn't you?" Chili said. "That alone could get you the fellowship."

"But to say I could identify the Gears? What am I going to do?"

Chili flashed me a grin. "Logan, you *can*. And she did come right out and say you could write the column. Maybe she won't even tell anyone you're going after the Gears."

"Right," Paige said, and got in back. "But we are going to need those gemstones more than ever."

I'd read that each sign has its own stone, so we were headed for a store that sold a variety of them. The black leather book had taken up permanent residency in my backpack. Once I consulted it again, I figured out that Paige, the Pisces, was the one who needed the purple stone. It was also supposed to help overcome escapism, and I had to admit, Paige spent considerable time in her private dreamworld.

Chili went for the brown tourmaline. It was supposed to help her filter all of the information she loved to collect.

"And besides," she said, and clasped the chain around her neck, "it looks hot on me."

I selected an aquamarine, which was supposed to help my squirrelly Aquarius self feel comfortable in social situations without having to compromise my own behavior.

Chili insisted on paying with Stella's credit card. Only one little problem. The card was rejected for being expired.

"How can that be?" Chili demanded, and waved it in the face of the clerk, a wimpy guy whose pale skin and soft voice reminded me of Charles Bellamy. "The expiration date is two years from now."

"We've been having some computer problems today," the clerk replied.

"Mercury." I reached into my bag, grateful I hadn't spent all the cash my dad had given me. "For once, let me pay."

"So what do we do while we wait for my hair appointment?" Chili asked once we were outside, our new pendants in place.

"Recheck, recharge, reflect," I said.

"Meaning?"

"That's what you do when Mercury is in retrograde. You check everything in your life twice, especially the mechanical stuff. It's a good time to shop, though."

"All right," Chili said.

"And to do research. Maybe we could get a cup of coffee and see what the stars have to say about our good friend Kat."

"Mercury can't be doing her any favors either," Chili said. "So where for coffee?"

"Let's go to Java & Jazz." Paige pointed at the coffee shop to our left. "It's so much cooler than the chains."

We walked in, and I realized she was right. The lights were dim, and tinkly low-pitched music softened the buzz of conversation. Just then I recognized this blue-haired guy named Hunter Allen behind the counter, his tattooed right arm catching the light like a stained-glass window. He looked up and flashed Paige a sexy grin.

Chili glared at her. "Did you know he'd be here?"

Paige replied with a helpless "Yes."

"So that's why you're dressed so hot," I said. "Don't tell me you're crushing on Hunter Allen."

"I'm afraid so. Pretty hopeless, isn't it?"

"I don't know about that," Chili said, "but he's in college."

"Junior college, and he's only a freshman."

"Well, he's still too old for you. Besides, you'd have to quit school and get a job just to keep him in tattoos."

"Don't tease." She reached for her coffee and gave Chili that Pisces *had-enough* look.

"If I can figure out Trevor for you," I said, "I can figure out tattoo man for Paige."

"All right." Chili grinned and started toward the back of the shop. Over her shoulder, she said, "But be careful what you wish for, Paige. Who knows what his hidden tats look like?"

The two of them settled on a sofa, and I pulled a chair close to the other side of the table.

"Well?" Paige asked me.

"The coffee is great," I told her.

Chili held her cup in both hands. "The book, Logan," she

said. "Give it up."

I read and highlighted. Paige took notes, and Chili crossed and uncrossed her arms against her chest as if trying to contain her energy.

"Well," I finally said, "Kat's an Aries."

"Meaning?" Chili demanded.

"She's not going to give up without a fight. Baby of the zodiac. *I, I, I. Me, me, me.* High drama, and what the book calls highly, uh, sexed."

Her eyes widened. "Do you think they slept together?"

"Wait, Chili," I said. "That describes only pure Aries. She could have a very cool and mellow Moon."

"All right, so find it already."

I flipped to the chart in the back of the book. Ran my finger down the column. Oh, no. Aries Moon too.

No wonder that hot-tempered little cheerleader had thrown such a public fit that night after open house.

My finger pressed against the revealing truth. "She's a double Aries, Chili," I said.

She looked stunned. "So all of that *I, I, I, me, me, me* and highly sexed stuff is twice as bad?"

"Something like that."

"So what do we do?"

"Figure out a way for you to appeal to the Scorpio in Trevor, maybe."

She tapped the side of her coffee cup. "And how's that?"

"Could she give him something?" Paige suggested with

that look she got when trying to figure out a math problem. "You said Geminis are generous, and we know Chili is."

"She can't just bounce up and shove a gift in his face." I didn't think this was the proper time to mention that the Gemini-Scorpio attachment seldom lasted longer than a six-pack after a Friday night football game.

"What if I gave him *back* something he gave me?"

"You have something of his?" Paige asked.

Chili giggled. "Just a stupid hoodie."

"Where'd you get it?" I asked.

"I *found* it at the swim party last summer. I guess he forgot it, and somehow it ended up in my backseat."

"Ew." Paige made a face. "That sweaty blue thing? I think I sat on it."

"I hope you washed it," I said.

Chili's cheeks flushed. "Anyway, do you think it's a good idea?" she asked. "I could say I just discovered it, and maybe we can meet somewhere so I can give it back to him."

"Laundered, of course." Paige made a face.

"Of course."

"You could also say that you sympathize with him about the situation with Kat," I said. "Scorpios sometimes don't want to let go of the past."

"Sympathize, my ass." She slammed a palm on the table.

"That type of Gemini, er, *spontaneity* doesn't much appeal to Scorpios," I told her. "The Scorpion is big on sympathy and empathy and short on blame and outbursts."

"Then they better learn. *Trevor* better." She struck the table again, and the coffee cup bounced into her lap.

"Ouch," she said, and jumped up.

Paige leaped to her feet and started dabbing at Chili's jumper with a napkin, oblivious to the flying drops just missing her own pale yellow skirt.

"What's wrong with me today?" Chili wailed.

"Mercury in retrograde." I stood up so fast that I almost knocked over my own coffee. "And you know what that means, don't you, girls?

"Recheck, recharge, reflect," we said in unison.

We were getting ready to leave when I realized I had a text message.

"Well, at least one mechanical object is working right today," I said.

> miss u

I actually gasped.

"Nathan?" Chili whispered.

I nodded. Managed to reply.

> miss u 2

> c u monday after school?

The essay needed to be finished. That's the one commitment I couldn't drop.

> time????

right after

have 2 talk 2 fstein

cool after that?

I got up and slowly put the cell phone in my backpack. Could this really be happening? Was I the same person who felt so helpless and miserable a couple of weeks ago?

Chili grabbed my arm. "Whatever you're doing, I hope you teach me how."

"Me too." Paige took hold of the other arm, and we walked out of the shop, but not before Paige waved good-bye to Hunter.

"I will," I said. "You know I will."

Then I glanced over my shoulder. Hunter stood watching us, watching Paige, with a look so intense that I knew he had to be a fire sign.

NOTES TO SELF

Even while I was dodging flying coffee today, I knew why Paige and Chili were so giggly. They now totally believe in the book's ability to help them change their lives too. Yes, I might as well admit, I believe it too, in a way I haven't believed in anything, including myself, for so long.

13

DON'T EVER DISCOUNT TAURUS. EVEN THOUGH BULLS TEND TO ACCEPT PEOPLE AND THINGS AT FACE VALUE AND CAN BE FOOLED, THEY ARE FAR FROM STUPID. THEY JUST LIKE TO TAKE THEIR TIME, AND WHEN THEY FINALLY DO MAKE A DECISION, IT CAN BE FOR-EVER. YOU CAN'T STAY CLOSE TO A TAURUS BY TRYING TO BE SMARTER. YOU CAN'T STAY CLOSE TO A TAURUS BY TRYING TO FLATTER, DISTRACT, OR CONFUSE. THE ONLY WAY YOU CAN POSSIBLY HOPE TO GET CLOSE TO THIS DOWN-TO-EARTH, PRACTICAL SIGN IS TO MAKE THAT BULL CARE.

—Fearless Astrology

The news spread fast. I was going to write an astrology-themed column. And I was going to ID the Gears. Thank you, Geneva! Add gossip hound to Libra's list of invisible flaws.

That Monday, Frankenstein and I sat across from each other at his desk after class. Behind his smudged glasses, his pale blue eyes were clear and something close to friendly. He might almost be enjoying the attention, which wasn't at all Taurus. A Leo Moon, perhaps?

"Let's make it fast," he said. "Astrology isn't my thing and isn't what I'd like to see you writing. I told Ms. Snider so."

"It's just for fun," I said. "Lots of papers do it."

"And you really think you are going to be able to identify those troublemakers?"

So he'd heard it too. "I'm going to do my best," I said.

He leaned forward, interested. "You do that, McRae, and you'll have something fresh to write about."

Of course. Identify the Gears, write about the experience, and blow away the other kids and their lame essay topics.

"You'd let me write about it?" I asked.

"I absolutely think you ought to. Whether or not you can find out who they are, it's a unique topic, and one I can see you care about."

Care was an understatement. And I *would* find out who they were, especially now that I knew he was intrigued by what I was doing.

"First, I need to finish this interview," I said. "I'm just

going to read from my list of Taurus traits, and you can tell me which ones are the most like you. The first one is a love for possessions."

He raised an eyebrow. "Are you asking if I'm a pack rat?"

I forced myself to stay calm and quiet. *Pack rat* was the actual term the book used.

"A lot of people like to hang on to keepsakes," I said. Make that *Taurus* people, but I didn't dare. "What's one of your favorites?"

"I don't know. I have so many." He looked down at his short-clipped fingernails. "Maybe a drawing of our family my son made when he was in kindergarten last year."

Even though Paige had, by way of her aunt, already clued us in about the divorce, I figured I should fake ignorance.

"I didn't know you had a son."

"His picture's right here."

He turned the framed photograph around. A cute little boy grinned back. The photo appeared to have been cut in half.

"He's adorable."

"Lives in Washington now. Next question?"

I felt as if I'd stepped into a mud puddle and tried to yank my foot out.

"Most of the people born under your sign are extremely successful," I said. "So, what do you feel is your greatest accomplishment?"

"Probably my athletic career. And being a dad, of course." His face flushed, and he toyed with the frame on the desk.

I could see that he was disturbed and reminded myself what the book said about Taurus and love. It was simple enough. Once in a relationship, even a bad one, a Taurus doesn't like to call it quits.

"All right, then." I tried to think of a less emotional subject. "Since you were an athlete, why are you teaching English and drama?"

"English minor," he said. "After my knee injury in college, I figured I didn't want to be just one more coach living through his students." I felt the tension leave the room. "You know what 'off the record' means, McRae?"

"Of course." Did he think I was a complete idiot just because I had problems getting *personal* in my essays?

"Every failed college athlete will tell you about the injury that ruined his career. The truth is that most of us just weren't that good."

"So you don't think the injury ruined yours?" I asked.

"At the time, I did, but look how many athletes get hurt and keep on going." He leaned forward and looked into my eyes. "What I just told you, McRae. That's what you have to do when you write your essays. You have to look at both sides of a situation. Don't just opt for the easy answer or emotion."

"How can I do that when I'm supposed to write about subjects that don't interest me? A fictional character I'd want to have lunch with, for instance." It was the topic of our next essay assignment, and I hadn't even been able to start it. "Why would I want to have lunch with someone who isn't real?"

"To find out how you feel and what you value. On some level, all writing is an act of discovery, you know."

That didn't sound so scary. For a moment, I thought about saying I'd pick Frankenstein or his monster, but I was pretty sure he knew about his nickname. Maybe I could pick Zeus and explain how the Greeks thought he was Taurus the Bull.

"Thanks for the help," I said. "I think I can do it. Part of my problem is that you're the first English teacher I've had who's been so, well, creative in your assignments."

"The next one's going to be author's choice, and you really should consider writing about your quest to identify the Gears." He glanced up at the clock. "Now, is my interview over?"

I panicked. I'd barely started. "Not quite." I handed him the list of traits. "Just pick a couple that sound like you, and we can wrap it up."

"I told you I don't believe in this stuff," he said. "But all right, let's see. I don't like to make fast decisions. That's just good sense. And I don't believe in something I can't touch, taste, or see. Astrology, for example. Be sure you put that in the article."

"I will," I said. "And even though you don't believe in astrology, that opinion is consistent with your sign."

"You are hardheaded, McRae. I'm proud of you, though."

That stopped me. "You are?"

"Yeah, I am." He pushed back his chair and gave me a grin. "It's not easy to get a column, and not easy to write one every other week. Says a lot about you that you're willing to pull it off. Strengths that you can draw on later."

Frankenstein was impressed. *By me*! I wasn't sure about the strengths-to-draw-on stuff, but I was liking this conversation.

"Thanks." I tried to stay calm, but it was all I could do to keep from bouncing around like Chili.

"It's so important to be able to rely on yourself, McRae. Important to know who you are."

I sensed someone at the door and looked up, almost relieved to break away from his intensity. It was Snider in a pale ivory tank and cropped jacket. In her hand was a folder. Printed on it in large letters was *Monterey Fellowship*. She stopped for a moment as if not sure whether or not to come into the room. So she must be one of the members of his secret committee.

Finally, she said, "Sorry. I was just going to leave this for you on my way to class. I didn't know you two were still working."

"No. Work's what I'm *not* doing," he blustered, and got up from his desk in one defiant gesture.

"Well, I'm sure you'll catch up." She shot me an inquiring look. "Are you about finished here, Logan?"

"I think so." I smiled at Frankenstein, trying not to think about what might be in that folder. "Thanks for being my first interview."

"Sure." He looked at Snider. "Got a minute?"

"Sorry," she said. "I have a class waiting."

We left but not before I caught the expression of defeat on his face. Was it possible? Yes, there was no mistaking the sad-dog look. Frankenstein was hot for Snider.

I did it," Chili shrieked into the hall. "I gave Trevor his hoodie." She hugged me. "You are so wonderful, Logan. I didn't even have to ask about Kat. He told me it was over and apologized for leaving the way he did at open house."

"That's great," I said.

"How did you do? Enough information to write a friendly piece about you know who?"

"I think so."

Make that hope so. Make that stunned about what I just figured out about Frankenstein. Although he was the one who kept pushing me to reveal myself in my writing, he'd revealed himself to me back there. Who would have guessed? Frankenstein had feelings too.

Nathan was waiting for me in the parking lot. I climbed into the Civic, and he grabbed my hand.

"I brought coffee," he said.

I took the cup, noticed it was from Java & Jazz, and tried to think of something Leo-flattering to say.

"You're really thoughtful, Nathan. Thanks."

"I didn't know you'd be so long. I hope it's not too cold."

Lukewarm, but I sipped it happily. Yes, he was a Leo, with

a vain Libra Moon, no less, but somewhere in all of that star stuff was a decent, caring guy.

"What are you thinking?" he asked.

I met his eyes and said, "Something nice about you."

"Tell me."

"Not right now."

"Later, then?" He squeezed my hand. "I need to get to drama rehearsal. Just wanted to see you before then. It's going to be a busy week."

Could life get any better? The boy I liked was happy to hold my hand and drink coffee, just so we could spend a few minutes together.

⁂

When my dad worked extra late, the plan was almost always for me to sleep over at Chili's. That night, her parents were going to a party, and no way would Stella allow us to stay by ourselves. Instead, we ended up at Paige's.

Although her mom didn't cook and fuss over us the way Stella did, she made sure there was plenty of food, and she asked that we respect her rule to be in bed before midnight. Other than that, she left us alone.

Paige's bedroom had a loft with a television. In the room below were two bunk beds and a wrought-iron dress form Paige had bought from a fabric store. Sometimes she put a hat on its neck. Tonight she'd strewn a long string of fake pearls around its lattice throat.

Even though it was almost as tall as we were, Paige treated her mannequin like a paper doll.

"You've got to give that dress form a name," Chili said.

"Why?" Paige asked.

Good question. Chili was the one who named everything from her car—which for reasons she refused to reveal was Roger—to her computer, which was Hap, for IIP.

"Because." Chili squirmed beside me on the side of the bunk. "She's one of us now, and if she could speak, just imagine the stories she could tell."

"Okay." Paige patted the thing on the shoulder and looked at me. "Can you come up with an astrological name for her, Logan?"

"Well . . ." I got up and walked around the room. "What's her best feature, other than the tiny waist, of course?"

"She can keep a secret," Paige said.

"Because she doesn't have a mouth." Chili giggled.

"Okay, so we need something that symbolizes silence. Isn't there a goddess?" I glanced at Paige, who'd moved protectively close to the nameless object. "Come on, you must know."

She gave it an affectionate pat and headed for her computer. "All I need are some keywords," she said.

"Goddess of silence."

"Done." *Click, click.* She squinted at the screen, lifted her glasses, and squinted again. "I've got it."

"What?" Chili and I shouted in unison.

"Calypso."

"That's silent?" Chili looked at me for clarification.

"Just listen," Paige said. "Calypso is the Greek goddess of silence, daughter of Atlas. Furthermore, she was part of *The Odyssey* because she hooked up with Odysseus on her island and kept him there for a time."

"Nasty thing," I said, and slapped our new friend on her out-of-proportion butt.

"Leave her alone." Paige got up and yanked my new favorite beret from my head. Then she plopped it down on the headless neck and said, "Welcome, Calypso. May you live up to the promise of your name."

Paige and I both applauded. We'd settled that one.

She and Chili went up to the loft so I could work without interruption. Except for a giggle now and then, I was able to do just that.

The Frankenstein Star Crossed interview almost wrote itself. After I finished, I took out *Fearless Astrology* again and read more about the Taurus Sun.

Once I figured a way to get Frankenstein's time and place of birth, I'd have even more to go on, but based on what I was reading, Taurus was almost the perfect sign for the head of the fellowship committee my future depended on. Being fair was a good thing, and it appeared that was almost a universal Taurus trait. And being slow to make a decision was a good thing. It would give me more time to try to convince him I was the student he had to give the best rec to.

If I could really figure out the Gears, that would help. He'd made it clear he thought that I should write about my search for them and had called it a fresh topic. Taurus was persistent too. I knew that if I were Frankenstein's choice, he'd make sure I got the fellowship.

I heard a creak-creak on the steps leading down from the loft. Paige and Chili tried to tiptoe into the room.

"Hey, guys," I said. "I'm still awake."

"Did you finish your column?" Chili asked.

"Yes, I did," I said. "And I also found out more stuff about Frankenstein's Sun sign."

"Have you figured out a way to get the Monterey thing?" Paige asked.

"Maybe," I whispered, and put my finger to my lips.

"And Trevor for me?" Chili whispered too.

Paige grabbed her arm. "All of us?" she asked.

"All of us, everything we want," I said. "Including a butt like Geneva's."

"You rock," Chili said. "What's next?"

"I'm not sure," I told her. "Frankenstein thinks I ought to write about finding the Gears. But before I can write about it, I have to do it."

She and Paige were quiet for a moment. Then Chili spoke. "And you know how?"

"Not a clue," I said, and we all laughed. "But I've got to try to figure it out."

NOTES TO SELF

The old me would never have been this confident, but I am no longer the old me. I am going to be a columnist, author of Star Crossed. Can't wait to tell Mom. No, don't go there, not tonight. I can't let myself think about how much I miss her.

Instead, just think about how I'm going to identify the Gears, about how Frankenstein will see that I really do deserve the fellowship. If my name isn't already in that folder Snider handed him, *Fearless Astrology* will get me there. Sun signs are starting to make sense to me now, and I know how to figure out Moon signs too. My next step is what the book calls "forecasting." Instead of wondering when the Gears will strike next, I'm going to let the stars predict it.

LUNCH WITH CALYPSO

1st Draft

Goddess of Silence, what would you do right now, and what would you say if you were in my place? You seem to have it going on, Calypso. And, as you may have noticed, I do not.

If we could meet for burgers or pizza, maybe you would finally break your silence. Perhaps you could teach me how you did what you did. How you kept that man as long as you did. How you survived after. You might even teach me how to forget.

LUNCH WITH CALPYSO

Final Draft

When considering fictional characters I'd like to know better, I decided on the mythical Calypso. There are many reasons for this decision. Perhaps studying her role in the strongest of the surviving epic tales might make her more real to me. As Joseph Campbell wrote . . .

Damn, I was doing it again.

14

THE WORD EPHEMERIS IS LATIN AND COMES FROM THE
GREEK WORD EPHÉMEROS, -ON, MEANING "DAILY." USE
THIS ALMANAC TO NOTE THE DAILY MOTIONS OF THE
PLANETS AND STARS. ALTHOUGH NO ONE CAN PREDICT
THE FUTURE, THE EPHEMERIS IS OUR BEST TOOL FOR
KNOWING WHAT TO EXPECT.

—Fearless Astrology

turned my Calypso piece in to Frankenstein,
cringing as I did so. It wasn't right, but I had no ideas
how to fix it. Maybe he would just focus on my column.
How could he hate something that was all about him?

The journalism staff was on deadline, and I stayed late
along with everyone else. Sure, I would have loved to stick
around and see the first printed copy—not to mention my
Star Crossed column—tomorrow morning instead of having

to wait until it was delivered on Monday. But I couldn't. We had planned our San Francisco weekend with Stella months ago, and it wouldn't be fair to cancel now.

Chili's folks leased a cool apartment in the Embarcadero District because her dad never missed a ball game, and Stella never missed an opportunity to shop. Ever since junior high, she had taken Paige, Chili, and me with her in the spring. It was a tradition we looked forward to, like celebrating one another's birthdays.

When I was done that Friday night, I left the journalism classroom. My dad had let me drive the dreaded van, and I was glad no one was around to watch me climb into it.

"Hey, um, Logan."

Strike that last thought. Someone *was* around. Geneva. Her green cashmere scarf had slid around the collar of her lavender jacket.

"Hi." I made a quick check of the lot and was thrilled that her car wasn't all that close to mine.

"You're really good," she said. "The column, I mean."

"Thanks." *Now leave me alone so I can get out of here before you see my pathetic van, if you haven't already.*

"What are you going to do next? Try to figure out who the Gears are, right?"

"Kind of," I said, "but in reverse. I'm going to use what's called an ephemeris to forecast the month. That will show us when they're most likely to strike again."

"The whole month?" She took a step back, and I realized it

was because we'd already passed her car. "Um, can you also figure out the best days for romance?"

Oh, yes.

"I think so," I said.

"Well, don't forget Libra when you're doing those calculations." She flashed me a sly smile I wished I could slap off her face.

Don't be jealous, I reminded myself. *She can't help it if she's gorgeous and hot for Nathan.*

"I won't," I said, "but most important is figuring out who the Gears are."

"Oh, right," she said. "Right."

I got out of there as fast as I could.

⁓⁓⁓

Later that night, after we arrived at the Chiliderians' San Francisco apartment, Chili, Paige, and I sneaked into the spare bedroom with the computer in it.

Stella was in her room chatting on the phone with her sister. They were first-generation Armenians and spoke to or saw each other every single day. I couldn't help comparing their closeness to my own family. It was okay that my mom followed her dreams, so why did it hurt like hell? There didn't seem to be a right answer for us or a road map to follow.

At least I had an astrological road map tonight. *Fearless Astrology* had been written long before the Internet, so I did not have to go through an old-fashioned ephemeris for my first attempt at predictive astrology. I could do it online.

I found an online version of the ephemeris that showed all the planetary positions for six thousand years. Six thousand? Wow. What would I learn about the tiny little rest of the month that was staring me in the face? I could hardly contain my excitement.

After I booted up the computer, they gathered around me.

"So what you're doing will predict the whole month?" Chili asked.

"Not predict exactly," I said. "It will only forecast when certain things are more likely to happen."

"Things like Mercury in retrograde?" Paige asked.

"Mercury," Chili said with a shudder. "Thank goodness that's over."

"Well, actually it lingers for a few days after."

"Oh, wonderful. What other lovely surprises do we have in store?"

"Well, the new moon on the fifth is a Gemini Moon. That's good for fresh starts, hatching new ideas, and making plans. Especially good for you, Chili."

"Good how? Will Trevor finally say what's on his mind?"

If she kept on with that, we'd be here all night, and I'd never be able to figure out the Gears.

"Whatever happens will be about starting fresh," I said. "Might as well be Trevor."

"Any Pisces moons?" Paige got up and moved closer to the

computer. "What's that on the screen over there? It has my Fish symbol."

"It's called a *glyph*," I said. "What's happening here is Venus moving into Pisces, and that's a good thing for you."

But I wasn't looking for good anything. I was looking for areas of the greatest strife so that I could track the Gears.

"Good *how*? Will Hunter finally notice me?"

"You have a pretty positive window there," I said. "Venus transits about three to four weeks."

"What's *transits*?" Chili asked.

"Moves," I said. "When she does, she ups the charm factor and attracts people to whatever sign she's in, which as of Monday will be the Fish here."

"Go, Pisces," Paige said.

"There's something else happening after that. A Mars in Pisces transit that will last about a month to six weeks could make you much more assertive."

"Cool."

Chili eased herself onto the chair beside me.

"Yes, cool," I said. "Now, girlfriends, I need to finish this."

"You're right." But Chili didn't budge. "If you catch the Gears, Logan, everything else will take care of itself."

"Exactly," I said, and peered at the screen, my heart racing. "On the fifteenth, there's going to be an Aries Moon, which can be pure trouble. The book calls it *raising mischief*. That could be the day."

"Are there any other possibilities?" Chili asked.

"Maybe here." I tapped the twenty-fifth. "It looks like a period of tense energies."

I realized that Paige had moved behind my chair and both girls were intently studying the screen.

"You're amazing, Logan," Chili said. "Do you realize the power you have?"

"Yeah," I finally said. We were all silent for a second. Motionless. Then we burst into squeals and hugs. Chili almost slid off the chair, but I managed to pull her up. "Yeah," I repeated. "I do."

NOTES TO SELF

The fifteenth and the twenty-fifth. These are the danger days. I couldn't have begun to figure that out a month or even a week ago. Even though I think Frankenstein is pretty much on my side now, he's going to be more so when he sees how hard I worked on the column about him. Imagine how impressed he and everyone else will be if I can really expose the Gears.

15

IF YOU'VE ANGERED A TAURUS, CONGRATULATIONS ON
YOUR PERSEVERANCE. IT'S NOT AN EASY FEAT, AND
YOU DESERVE EVERY MOMENT OF WHAT IS GOING TO
HAPPEN NEXT. IT WILL TAKE A LOT OF TAUNTING FOR A
BULL TO GO INTO BATTLE. BUT THEN, LOOK OUT. WAVE
THAT RED FLAG LONG ENOUGH, INSULT OR EMBARRASS
THE PEACE-LOVING TAURUS, AND YOU ARE GOING TO
HAVE A WAR ON YOUR HANDS. ONE YOU ARE PROBABLY
NOT GOING TO WIN.

—*Fearless Astrology*

The whole time we were in San Francisco, I thought
about what I'd learned. If I were correct, I might be
able to predict the next Gears attack. In addition, we'd
identified the ideal romance times for Paige, Chili, and yes, for

me. (*Darn.* Guess I forgot to check Libra. Sorry, Geneva.)

Some guy at the Beat Museum started checking Chili out, and Stella mother-henned us to the safety of Nordstrom. As usual, she wanted to buy everything in the city for us, but we weren't that into it, not even Chili. I think we all sensed how important it was to get back home.

Finally, we were, and finally, it was Monday. Good-bye, Logan. Hello, Star Crossed.

"Why so quiet?" Chili asked on our way to school that morning.

"Just thinking about the column."

"It will be fabulous," Paige said.

"I hope I'm there when he sees it for the first time. He is so going to love it."

"Are you starting to like Frankenstein?" Chili asked as we pulled into the school parking lot.

It was a simple question, but I couldn't answer it. I was still kind of afraid of him, but he'd been nice to me. Knowing that he was hot for Snider—something I hadn't told anyone— somehow made him more human. Maybe the article would show Snider his sensitive side. Maybe they'd get together, and he'd be so grateful that he'd personally call the college in Monterey, and . . .

"Logan?" Chili shook my arm.

I realized that she and Paige had been staring at me while I was picturing his undying gratitude. Daydreaming. Must be my Pisces Moon.

"Sorry," I said. "My mind was drifting."

"I asked you if you're starting to like Frankenstein." She said it the way she might ask if I was starting to like canned peas.

"Chili, please."

"It's all right if you are. Paige and I just need to know, is all, so that we can like him too." She made a face. "Or at least not trash him anymore."

"Well, he's a Taurus," I said.

"And that's a good thing?"

I nodded. "Can be. Often is."

"Then why's he so, you know? And do we like him, or don't we?"

"Yeah," I said. "I think we do."

I went directly to Frankenstein's room. Just as I imagined, he sat at his desk the newspaper in his hands.

I stepped into the room in the khaki sweater Chili and Paige said matched my eyes.

"Hi," I said, and waited for the kudos I knew would follow.

Honestly, it wasn't even about the praise anymore. Sure, I wanted the fellowship as much as ever, but I also just wanted to see that usually surly Frankenstein face happy for a change.

He looked up slowly, and I could tell that I was the last person on earth he wanted to see just then.

"What's going on?" he demanded. "What have you done?"

I rushed to the front of the room and took the newspaper he handed me. There it was, just as we'd laid it out. Everything looked fine—except my column.

My mouth went dry, and my whole body went numb. My mind tried to unscramble the cruel joke I was holding in my hand. Someone had photoshopped devil horns on Frankenstein's photo. And the article I'd worked on almost as many hours as I'd spent going over *Fearless Astrology* was no longer an article, only a series of words. Make that one word.

devildevildevildevil
devildevil
devildevildevildevil
devildevildevil
devildevildevildevildevildevil
devildevil devildevil
devildevil

And so on. That's right. Someone had completely destroyed my column. Trashed it. All that remained of the original piece was my byline. Frankenstein had a right to be furious. But so did I.

"I didn't have anything to do with this," I said.

"Then who did?"

I couldn't stay and argue with him.

"I don't know," I said, and started for the door. "But I'm going to find out."

"Wait."

"Sorry. I can't. I've got to talk to Snider."

With that, I left him and ran down the hall to the journalism classroom, remembering that I'd forgotten the *Ms.* in *Ms. Snider*. Oh, well.

When I burst into the room, I heard a gasp and realized it came from Snider herself. Clearly she'd just seen the paper. Sol from Texas sat with a stunned, frozen expression. Geneva and Charles sat side by side, Geneva's face in her hands, Charles shocked and wide-eyed.

"What's the meaning of this?" Snider demanded. "Logan, what happened? Why?"

"She didn't do it." Geneva lifted her head. Her expression was pained. "I know she didn't, Ms. Snider. Logan and I left together Friday night."

"That's the truth," I said. "I was in San Francisco all weekend, and I can prove it."

"You don't have to prove anything to me," Geneva said. "I watched you get into your, um, vehicle that night."

Rub it in, Libra, even during a crisis.

"You saw the layout," I told her. "Who touched it after we did?"

"Only the print shop."

"And after that?" I looked toward the sound of the voice and realized that Frankenstein had followed me into the room. "I want to know who touched this newspaper after Logan and Geneva left on Friday."

"Only the print shop," Geneva repeated. "They process on Friday and deliver on Monday."

"*Who* delivered?" Frankenstein demanded.

Geneva turned slowly to Charles. His voice was barely audible.

"Please," he moaned.

"I'm sure he's innocent," Geneva said. "Just because he was the last person to see the newspaper doesn't mean that he'd . . ."

For a moment I thought Frankenstein was going to grab Charles.

"Wait." I stepped between them. "He wouldn't."

"Well, who would?" His eyes were wild, like the Bull he was.

"Who do you think?" I looked around the room at all of them, saw the anger in Frankenstein's face, the fear in Charles's expression.

"The Gears?" Charles whispered the question.

"Exactly," I said. "I know Charles didn't have anything to do with this, Mr. Franklin."

"The Gears," Charles repeated, his voice stronger now.

"They did it," I told him, "and they set you up to take the blame."

"I realize that now," he said. "But who's going to believe me?"

"I'm not," Frankenstein bellowed. "Not until you answer a few questions."

NOTES TO SELF

I'm writing this down fast in the restroom because I promised to meet Charles in the hall. He didn't mess up my column, I know that. The Gears did. And they did it to hurt me. Why, though? They must think I'm getting too close to figuring out who they are! I need to clear my head and do a quick search for troublemakers. Here I spent all weekend trying to forecast danger days, and I didn't even realize there was one waiting for me as soon as I got home.

FIRE SIGNS ARE NOT THE ONLY DISRUPTIVE ONES; THEY ARE ONLY THE MOST OBVIOUS. ARIES, LEO, AND SAGITTARIUS EACH HAVE DIFFERENT REASONS FOR BEING BAD. ARIES IS RULED BY MARS, THE GOD OF WAR. SOME RAMS WOULD RUN DOWN THE STREET NAKED IF THEY COULD. LEO, RULED BY THE SUN, WAS BORN IN THE LIMELIGHT, AND THE LION INTENDS TO STAY THERE, NO MATTER WHAT. LEO WANTS ATTENTION BECAUSE HE THINKS HE DESERVES IT. SAGITTARIUS IS RULED BY JUPITER AND FEARS COMMITMENT ALMOST AS MUCH AS HE CRAVES ADVENTURE. THE ARCHER RUNS IN ORDER TO STAY FREE. THESE ARE THE ACTION SIGNS, AND, YES, THEY CAN BE DANGEROUS. BEFORE YOU JUDGE, HOWEVER, LOOK AT THE WHOLE CHART. DON'T JUDGE A SIGN BY ITS SUN.

—Fearless Astrology

I was hoping the book would give me a clue, but from what I could tell, any sign could be disruptive. Standing at the basin in the girls' restroom, I ran my fingers over those tarnished stars. The answers were beneath the cover of this book. I needed to get better at finding them.

Just as he'd promised, Charles met me in the hall.

"Sorry to be late," he said. "Thanks for what you did in there."

"I didn't do anything."

"You told the truth. If you hadn't, I would have gotten blamed for what happened."

He was right. "I know. You were totally set up."

"Something was different that night." His voice was so soft that I could barely hear it.

"What do you mean, Charles?"

"After you and Geneva left, someone else came back," he said. "Said we needed to proof the pages again. I was all right with that. I should have been more careful."

"Who came back?" I asked.

He gave me a helpless look. "I can't tell you."

"Why?" I asked.

Color spread across his face.

"Well, I was kind of spending time with someone," he said.

What did he mean, *spending time with someone*? Was he trying to say he was with a girl? That was insane.

"I'm your friend," I said. "You know that, don't you?"

He nodded and said, "Yes."

I *was* his friend, wasn't I? When had that happened?

Maybe the first day Frankenstein gave him a hard time in class. The way he used to give me a hard time.

"You need to tell me who you were with Friday night," I said, "when you were supposed to be overseeing the printing of the newspaper."

"I can't." He looked down. "It's my fault this happened."

"It's not your fault, Charles. This is a Gears' job. You must know that."

"I just feel so stupid." His voice was miserable, and he looked so lost that I almost wanted to hug him.

"Come on," I said, and stepped into the library.

He followed reluctantly and continued to look at the floor.

"Mr. Franklin's going to get me kicked out of school," he said. "He's always hated me."

"I don't think that's the right word. I mean, I think it's been a difficult year for Mr. Franklin, with the divorce and all."

"He's divorced?" He glanced up at me, then quickly returned to his examination of the carpet on the floor.

"Since the end of last year," I said. "The only reason he's so angry with you at the moment is because he thinks you had something to do with what happened to my column. Tell me who you were with, and we can clear it all up right now."

Finally, he met my eyes. "I can't," he said.

"All right, then. I respect that you want to protect the person you were with. Could you tell me where you were when someone came back to proof the pages?"

He turned an even brighter shade. "In the copy room."

That little four-by-four closet with a copy machine and a bunch of foul-smelling chemicals the photo department stored in there? *Yuck.* What could he have been doing? No, I didn't even want to explore that one.

"You do realize that by protecting whomever you were with, you're protecting the Gears, don't you?"

"I'll take the blame if I have to." His attitude had changed from wimpy to almost defiant.

"Fine, if that's the way you feel. If you change your mind, let me know," I said. "I need to get to class."

"Wait." He reached out for my arm, got my sweater instead. "You've been really nice to me, Logan. Nicer than anybody, except Ms. Snider. If I told anyone, you'd be the one."

"Then think about it," I said. "Please think about it, for your sake as well as mine."

"I feel rotten that it was your column it happened to. You're the one person I think kind of understands me. You know what it's like to have a famous parent."

I could see through the window that it was starting to rain outside again, but I could tell that he hadn't noticed. And what was he trying to say about famous parents?

"Meaning?"

"Meaning I know it's not easy," he said, and I knew he was studying my face to gauge my reaction. "My dad was Charlie Bell."

"Charlie Bell, the race car driver?"

Make that crashed and dead race car driver, one of our

small town's heroes. How could quiet, nerdy Charles Bellamy be the son of Indy great Charlie Bell?

"Right," he said.

"Oh, Charles, I didn't know. I'm so sorry."

"He died doing what he loved." I could tell that he'd said this before any number of times. "My guardian is my mom's brother. Very few people know who my dad was."

"Where's your mom?"

He paused, then said as if reciting from a memorized script, "She has a hair salon in Beverly Hills. It's not the proper environment to raise a young man."

"Why are you telling me all this?" I asked.

Those pale eyes didn't blink, but I sensed the unshed tears there.

"Because it's not that different with you and me."

"But my mom's a golfer."

Not a suicidal, crazed race car driver, I thought.

"It's not that different," he repeated. "I need to go to class too. Thanks again."

I watched him walk out of the room but I couldn't let him go. There was something I needed from him first.

"Charles, wait." I ran after him and managed to catch him before he moved, without protection, into the sudden storm.

"What?" he asked.

"Your birth date," I said. "Give it to me, and you can have this."

I handed him my big fat black umbrella.

"You don't need to do that." He shoved it back in my hands. "The twenty-fourth of June, 5:25 P.M. Thanks again for trying to help."

I watched him walk out into the rain, bareheaded, and wondered what to do next. Why did Charles make me feel so sad?

NOTES TO SELF

Just figured it out. Charles is a Cancer—translation: emotional, mom-driven homebody—with a Scorpio/secret Moon. I never would have guessed he shares a Sun with Michael Phelps, Lindsay Lohan, Derek Jeter, and Prince William.

His focus is all about family, but from what I can tell, he doesn't have one, other than his uncle/guardian. He thinks we're alike, but I've got news for him: I have a family. Charlie Bell died in one of the most dramatic crashes in the history of the Indy 500. Maybe I'm making it up, but I can almost remember it. Can almost remember my mom saying, "Such a tragedy, such a good man." I can ask once she's home again. Once I have my mom back.

THERE'S MUCH POWER IN ARIES, AND THE RAM OFTEN EASILY OBTAINS THE DESIRED OBJECT OR PERSON, REGARDLESS OF WHETHER OR NOT IT'S THE BEST CHOICE. AN ARIES MOON CAN LEAD TO A READY TEMPER, EMOTIONAL OUTBURSTS, AND DOWNRIGHT CRUELTY. IT CAN ALSO LEAD TO HASTY DECISIONS, POOR CHOICES, AND SELF-SABOTAGING BEHAVIOR. IF YOU'RE DEALING WITH AN ARIES, JUST REMEMBER WHATEVER CRISIS IS HAPPENING RIGHT NOW WILL BE FORGOTTEN TOMORROW WHEN THE BABY OF THE ZODIAC IS ABSORBED ONCE MORE IN THAT WONDERFUL FASCINATION WITH SELF. WITH ARIES AS THE ASCENDANT (RISING SIGN), EVEN THE MEEKEST SUN SIGNS ARE EMBOLDENED. ARIES ASCENDANT TYPES ARE OFTEN CONSIDERED INDEPENDENT BY THOSE WHO

TRY TO CONTROL THEM. MORE ACCURATELY, THEY
TEND TOWARD BEING SELF-RELIANT AND ENTERPRIS-
ING. IF YOU HAVE AN ARIES RISING, UNDERSTAND
THAT ALTHOUGH YOU WANT TO FINISH FIRST IN EVERY
ENDEAVOR, YOU'LL BE HAPPIER IN THE LONG RUN IF
YOU CHOOSE YOUR BATTLES.

—Fearless Astrology

*A*ries Rising.

That was me all right. But how was I going to choose my battles when the battles kept choos-ing me? My Rising or Ascendant was supposed to be the way I reacted to new people or situations, and right now, it was to find out who had destroyed my article.

It wasn't Charles. That Cancer was clearly protecting someone, and it had to be someone he really cared about. From what I'd been able to tell, he didn't care about anyone but Ms. Snider. I had to find out. Once I did, I could go to Frankenstein and reveal the truth. And he'd be so grateful that he'd drive to Monterey, meet with his old friends, and tell them . . .

I didn't have time to daydream. I needed to figure out the Gears. Fire signs seemed the best place to start, especially since I'd narrowed down the danger days to May fifteenth and twenty-fifth.

Having gotten drenched in the rain, I dashed into the restroom to see if I could rescue my frizzy hair. The bangs really were an improvement. I pulled them down over my eyebrows. The rest of my hair was pretty hopeless.

A girl swooshed through the bathroom door. I barely looked up from the counter that ran along both sides of the sinks.

"Hey, Logan."

It was Kat in full cheerleader attire, which was what Snider would call, well, sparse. I remembered what I'd just read about Aries: *The Ram often easily obtains the desired object or person, regardless of whether or not it's the best choice.*

"Hi, Kat."

She was way too energetic and in no hurry to enter a stall. At first I thought she might have come in because it was warmer here than out wherever she was supposed to be jumping around. Then, with a chill, I realized she must have followed me inside.

"How are you doing?" she said in a perky voice.

"All right." I put my notebook into my book bag.

"It was fun painting sets with you and Nathan. You're really cute together."

Enough chitchat.

"What's up, Kat?" I asked.

She took a step back, and the fake smile disappeared from her face. "Well, I hear you're an expert on astrology."

Guess she hadn't seen the botched newspaper yet.

"I know a little bit about it."

"I understand you're really good." Her blue eyes, shiny from tinted contacts, widened even more. "Could you figure out something for me? It's about a guy, of course."

"Not right now," I said. "I'm in a hurry."

Not to mention, there was no way I would share any information with Chili's main competition for Trevor.

"How much?" Kat asked as if talking to a clerk in a shop.

"What do you mean?"

She was really irritating me now.

"What do you charge?" She put her hands on the hips of her crotch-length skirt. "I'll pay you whatever."

"I *don't* charge. And for your information, Nathan and I are just friends."

"That's not what he's saying. I don't know what kind of spell you put on him, but it worked." The fake smile was back in place. "And I want you to teach me how. I'm a quick study. It shouldn't take long."

"Astrology isn't magic," I said. "It doesn't have anything to do with casting spells." My heartbeat quickened. Was Nathan really talking about me? Saying that we were more than friends?

"All I know is that until a month ago, you were this shy, wimpy little sophomore," she said. "Now, one of the two hottest senior boys in school is after you, and everyone's saying you've got the power to bring down the Gears."

"One doesn't have anything to do with the other." I was so embarrassed that I wasn't sure what to say, let alone how to stop the sudden rush of heat to my cheeks. "Besides, I may not actually be able to bring down the Gears, as you so eloquently put it. And, Kat, there's no way I can help you. There really isn't."

"My jean jacket?" She said it like a question, as if she hadn't heard a word of what I'd just told her.

"What are you talking about?"

"You said you loved my jacket. Teach me how to keep a certain guy hot for me, and I'll give it to you."

"Are you serious?"

"My Coach purse too." She crossed her arms, and the smile got even scarier. "Do we have a deal?"

"We do not," I said. "I can't teach you how to keep Trevor hot for you."

Especially when you scream in his face in the school parking lot, you freak show.

Now she was the one with the red face.

"Come on. Everyone's talking about what you can do."

I picked up my backpack. "I've been lucky."

"Lucky doesn't get the kind of stuff you and your friend Chili have been getting." She looked in the mirror and fluffed her short bob. As she did so, the jacket rose over her back, revealing a tattoo that appeared to be her own initials. Then she turned and looked back at me over her perfect chest the way she might look at dirt.

"What do you mean?" I asked.

"That *lucky* would *not* get you Nathan Sullivan, Logan. Not in any lifetime."

Heat flooded my face. "What are you trying to imply?" I managed.

Her smile was as acidic as her voice. "I think you know as well as I do."

"Well, I've got to go, Kat. Nice talking to you."

"Don't you get what I'm trying to tell you?" Her voice rose, and I remembered the open house night in the parking lot. "I need your help."

"Kat," I said, "I'm leaving. Deal with it or don't. I'm out of here."

As I left the restroom, I could hear her yelling. *Don't you dare leave while I'm talking . . . Who do you think you are?*

Double Aries. The book was right again.

NOTES TO SELF

Was Kat telling the truth? Am I just an absolute loser who wouldn't have had a chance at Nathan without the help of astrology? Or did the book just give me an extra shot of courage? I can't worry about her nasty comments. I'm starting to fear the Aries sign, though, even though it is my own Ascendant, and I can't help wondering if it's the sign of at least one of the Gears.

18

WHILE AQUARIANS ARE SOME OF THE KINDEST AND
MOST GENTLE PEOPLE ON EARTH, THEY OFTEN ARE
FOUND IN THE MIDDLE OF CHAOS. FURTHERMORE, IT IS
THE NATURE OF AN AIR SIGN TO WANT TO KNOW WHY.
EVEN WHEN SOMEONE CAN GET AN AQUARIAN TO SHUT
UP, THE BRAIN WILL CONTINUE TO QUESTION. OTHERS
OFTEN DO NOT UNDERSTAND THAT AQUARIUS IS DRIVEN
TO SEEK ANSWERS AND SPEAK OUT FOR ANY CAUSE HE
BELIEVES IS JUST.

—Fearless Astrology

That was for sure. The more I got into the book, the
more I was acting like its description of Aquarius.
Almost as if *Fearless Astrology* was giving me
permission to be who I'd always been secretly. It was also
warning me about traits to watch—like being too detached,

for instance. For trying to *figure out* a situation before asking myself how I *felt* about it.

That night we were hanging out at Chili's, as usual, pretending to do homework. Actually, Paige was kind of doing it. Sitting cross-legged on the carpet in front of the French doors, she held an open history book and highlighted parts of it from time to time.

The girl had the rare ability to carry on a conversation and keep track of what she was reading at the same time. Next to her on the floor was an open fashion magazine, and I would not be surprised if she were stealing glances at it too.

When I told them about Kat's crazy antics, they were outraged.

"She's just jealous of both of us," Chili said. "Nathan would like you without the astrology. It's just kind of . . ."

"*Escalated* his interest in you," Paige finished, looking up from her book.

"And it sure escalated . . ." Chili giggled ". . . Trevor's interest in me. That's what Kat's really going nuts about."

"Wish it would escalate Hunter a little," Paige said.

Chili had managed to get Hunter's birthday from J.T., whose sister went out with him last year. "Just find out his exact time and place of birth, and I can do an in-depth chart. We know he's an Aries, and as Kat has demonstrated, that can mean a lot of hot-headed tantrums."

"Not Hunter," she said dreamily. "He's the sweetest, most soft-spoken . . ."

I thought about the tattoos and the musicians he hung out with.

"Well, maybe he's got a great Venus and Mars. The only way we can know that is if you figure out a way to get that information."

"How would I ask?" she said. "I can hardly speak around him."

"Aries are one of the easiest signs to approach, and they like to talk about themselves. Just ask."

"What if he asks why?"

"Okay, *I'll* talk to him," Chili said. "We have to find out, for your sake."

"I'd be too embarrassed."

"All right, all right." Chili began pacing the room in her tank and shorts the way she liked to when she was dreaming up a wild Gemini scheme. "I think I've got it. Logan, what if you had a drawing to give away a free astrological reading, and what if Hunter won it?"

Paige still looked worried. "Wouldn't he know? I mean, he's not even a student."

"Not if we had more than one winner. We could just say we had a drawing, and someone entered his name." As usual, I was getting caught up in Chili's excitement. "Maybe I could select a winner a week. I could do Frankenstein too. I still need more than his Sun and Moon. Of course, they wouldn't have any idea that it was for our own snoopy reasons."

"Brilliant," Chili said.

Just then, my cell phone began to chime.

I didn't recognize the number but answered it anyway. I'd been getting calls and e-mails from a lot of kids in school. This was probably just another one, like Kat, who thought I had the answers to all problems thanks to my supposed shortcut to the stars.

"Hey, Logan."

I didn't recognize the raspy voice and couldn't even tell if it was male or female.

"Who is this?"

"Lay off, Logan."

"What?" I couldn't believe what I'd just heard.

"Lay off, or look out."

Now I was mad.

"Lay off *what*?"

Chili and Paige gathered around me.

"What are they saying?" Chili whispered.

I shook my head and waited for the voice.

"Lay off the Gears."

"That will be a cold day in hell." One of my gram's antique clichés. It rolled out effortlessly. Like breathing.

"Lay off the Gears, or you don't want to know what will happen to you."

"And what's that?" I asked.

Silence for a moment, and then, "Try this."

Just then, something crashed through Chili's bedroom window. Shards of glass shattered everywhere.

We screamed.

Paige grabbed her foot, and I watched with horror as a tiny trickle of red bled through her white sock.

Chili jumped over the glass shards on the carpet to inspect Paige's injury.

I started to join her, then realized that I was still holding the phone to my ear.

"Hey, Logan. We're closer than you think."

The phone went dead just as Stella burst into the room.

"What happened?" she demanded. "Oh, honey, what's going on?"

I realized that she was looking at me.

"I'm not sure, Stella," I said. "But I think I'm the reason for it. I should go home."

"You're not leaving this house." She shoved her hands into the pockets of her faux leopard robe and stood in front of me. "Logan, honey, unless you're going to walk right through me, there's no way you're leaving here tonight."

Like the idiot that I was, I began to cry.

"It's all right." Stella pulled her hands out of her pockets and wrapped her arms around me.

"It's going to be fine." Chili's arms now. And Paige's.

Chili's dad burst into the room.

"Cops are on their way," he said. "Those little punks are not going to get away with this." Then he left to wait for the police.

I was scared, and worse, I felt like a failure. It wasn't the fifteenth and sure wasn't the twenty-fifth. I hadn't anticipated this. And I hadn't predicted the column sabotage either. If the big danger days were still ahead, I was in trouble.

I tried to trace the call, but somehow they had gotten past the caller I.D. "The Gears did this," I choked out. "And Paige got hurt."

"It's nothing," she said. "They scared me more than anything."

"Because they hate me."

"Well, we love you, honey." Stella refused to let me escape her tight embrace. "It's going to be all right."

"They didn't do it because they hate you." Chili shook my arm. "They did it because they're afraid of you, Logan."

"That's right." Paige looked down at her foot. "They know you can identify them."

Of course. "If they think I can do that, you know what that means?" I asked.

Chili's eyes grew wide. "It means you're close."

"Honey, I don't want you worrying about matters that it's up to the school and the police to solve." Stella put her hands on her hips and gave me that *mom* look.

"I understand," I said.

She hugged me again, and over her shoulder, I grinned at Chili and Paige. All the Gears could do was run naked, make anonymous phone calls, and throw rocks. They were afraid of me because I was close. And you know what? I was going to get even closer very soon.

NOTES TO SELF

Idiots. As much as they scared us, they gave away too much about themselves. They're the ones who are scared. Chili was right about that. And the book was right about this Aquarius and Aries Rising. There's no way I'm going to back down. In the meantime I have to ask Snider who to interview next. It's going to have to be a great interview to make everyone forget what happened to the first one.

19

Beneath the elegant surface, Capricorns are dry. Dry wit, sometimes even dry skin. Many Goats experienced a childhood lack of love or money and feel deprived and driven to build a secure financial future. They become less driven and more flexible as they age and all of their hard work begins to pay off. If you want to win over a Capricorn, make it clear that you're not afraid of hard work either. Then prove it.

—*Fearless Astrology*

Capricorn, Earth.

Capricorn, sign of Ryan Seacrest, Tiger Woods—and Ms. Snider.

Capricorn, the practical Goat.

Reading the Capricorn chapter was almost like peeking into Snider's journal—not that a Capricorn would waste her time on such an indulgence. I went down the list. Rich, earthy colors. *Check.* Understated elegance. *Check.* A need for praise. Now, that was a new one.

I wrote that down and made sure I got to journalism class a little early. Not early enough, as it turned out. Charles Bellamy was already there. He was standing as close to Snider's desk as possible, gazing up into her eyes. Bummer. I didn't want an audience when I told Snider what happened at Chili's.

Snider's olive green top had a square neck that played up her shoulders but in a classy way. She touched Charles on the arm and nodded. Whatever they were discussing had to be pretty intense. I wondered if I should leave the room and come back later.

"It's all right, Logan," Snider said, without looking up. "Take a seat, and I'll be right with you."

Charles whispered something to her and started to walk away from her desk. When he passed me, he flashed a sly little smile that almost made him cute. I thought about Charlie Bell, whom I'd already Googled. If Charles were not so shy, if he grew his blond hair a little longer, ditched the glasses, and talked a little more and a little louder . . . he would look a lot like his famous late father.

Just then, I realized why Charles was taking auto shop. Chili had said the two of them were the best students. She'd also said he could take apart a car's engine like no one she'd ever known. I'll bet Charles wanted to be like his dad. He probably thought he could drive like a champion as well, the way I once thought I could slam a golf ball across the course just because my mom could.

Oh, no. Had Charles been right when he said we weren't all that different?

He walked out of the room, and Snider approached me. Decent, I thought. When most kids would have just flopped down at their desk, Charles was cool about giving us some privacy.

"We're going to re-print the newspaper," Snider said. "Your column will run as it was originally written and laid out."

Visions of Frankenstein danced in my head. Happy Frankenstein. Appreciative Frankenstein. Thrilled-for-me-and-committed-to-my-summer-fellowship Frankenstein.

"Thank you," I said, and tried to find the courage to say the rest.

It was the truth, and I owed it to her.

She reached out, squeezed my shoulder. "What's the matter, Logan?"

"I got a threat last night," I told her.

"No."

"Afraid so. Someone called me when I was spending the night at Chili's house. Said it was the Gears and told me to lay off."

"How could you be sure it was the Gears?" she asked.

"Because they did more than just call. Someone threw a rock through the window. Paige got a cut on her foot, and Chili's dad had to call the police."

"Oh my goodness." She pulled a desk over and sat down in it next to me. "Mr. Chiliderian was right to call the police. There's no way you should be trying to identify the Gears right now."

"But I kind of promised Geneva. I don't want to lose the column."

"She'll understand," Snider said. "You can worry about the Gears later."

Why didn't she see how important this was, especially since the Gears had attacked her reputation? And, yes, I realized I was doing the Aquarius *why, why, why* thing.

"I already know when they're going to strike next," I said. "I have to try, Ms. Snider."

"You actually know?"

"I think I do."

"You can't, Logan. No one can." She leaned forward in the chair so close that I could smell her minty breath. "No writing about or investigating them until we learn more. Do you understand?"

"Don't you want to see them stopped?"

"Not if it puts a student in jeopardy."

I remembered what I'd read in the book about impressing Capricorns and said, "I'm willing to work hard to figure it out. As many hours as necessary."

She paused only momentarily, then shook her head and gave me that firm, icy look. "Spend all that time on your next column."

I didn't bother to protest. There was no way she could stop me from what I wanted to do, and no way to convince her.

"Which teacher should I write about?" I asked.

She shrugged and replied, "Your choice."

"What about you?"

"Me?" Her hand flew to the real-looking green stone in the pendant around her neck. "I'm the least-interesting teacher on campus. All I do is work."

"It will pay off," I said, remembering what I read.

Workaholic.

Secretly building wealth.

Focused.

Lonely.

Yes, she was probably lonely too.

"I'm sure it will." She ran her fingertip over the jewel around her neck. "We'd all like to reach the goals we set for ourselves."

"Many Capricorns feel that way." Why was I showing off? I wasn't sure. But I did want to help her, and, yes, impress upon her what a good job I could do with the column. "They build up huge savings accounts too."

She looked flustered and a little miffed. "How could you know anything about that?"

I'd shot my mouth off again and way too soon.

"A good guess?"

She bristled in the chair. "Security isn't just possessions, Logan, but that's probably something I should not be discussing with you. You need to find another teacher for your column. I'm way too boring."

"Not to me," I said.

She sighed. "Thank you for that. I have an idea, though. We need someone really positive and upbeat after what happened with the first column."

I wanted to say that she was positive and upbeat but knew that she wasn't going to allow me any further into her head. Didn't blame her. If I weren't already residing in my own head, I wouldn't want me poking around in there either.

"Why not interview Ms. Berry?"

Jillian Berry, the art teacher? Not one of my favorite people. "But I'd rather—"

"Trust me, Ms. Berry's a lot more fun than I am."

Fun meaning the really lame jokes Berry told in class and a mass of frizzy carrot-red hair that made even mine look smooth and normal. Fun meaning she took kids on field trips to galleries, lakes, and mountains. Fun especially meaning those nude paintings of hers that hung in local shops, and the way everyone in town wondered who the faceless men in them were.

"If you want me to interview Ms. Berry, I'll interview Ms. Berry."

"I do," she said in that strictly business way of hers.

And with that, I felt dismissed.

"Is something wrong?" Snider asked.

Oh, no, nothing's wrong, Snider. You ask me to avoid looking into the Gears. You ask me to interview Berry, who everybody calls Cherry Berry. That will be fun, all right.

"Not at all," I said. *Capricorn needs praise. Think praise.* "Thanks for taking all this time for me. I appreciate it."

NOTES TO SELF

I got so distracted trying to talk to Snider that I forgot to tell her about my new idea (well, Chili's) for people—two of whom will be Frankenstein and Hunter—to win free charts and consultations. It was so weird looking at Snider the way the book described her, listening to what she said—and didn't say. In spite of her insistence about the Gears, I am more convinced than ever that I have the ability to find out who they are. And, yes, I'm still convinced that they're planning something for the fifteenth. And still going to do my best to stop it.

Star Crossed

Focus on Mr. Franklin

Shakespeare was a Taurus—and so is this English teacher

With a passion for Shakespeare and what he calls "writing your truth," Mr. Franklin is the subject of our first Star Crossed scope.

Is it a coincidence that he shares a Sun sign with the guy he calls the bard?

"I don't believe in something I can't touch, taste, or see. Astrology, for example. Be sure you put that in the article."

Taurus trait: *Slow to change their minds.*

Raised by his mother, Mary, a widow with three sons, and a grandfather who was retired from the Marines, Mr. Franklin learned discipline at an early age.

"A sports scholarship got me out of there, and a knee injury got me out of that," he says. "I coached for a while, but when an opening for an English/drama teacher came along, I went for it."

He strives to teach students—and not just the English geeks—the importance of finding their voice.

"You've got to write your truth your way," he says. "Write as if everyone you know is dead. You can always edit later or just hit the delete key. But if you can't find your voice and speak your truth now, how difficult do you think it's going to be five or ten years from now?"

Taurus colors: *Blue, brown, yellow*

Check out those eyes—and that car

Taurus relationships: *Steady, long-term*

Students at Terra High will no doubt be reading Shakespeare and writing their truth in Mr. Franklin's classroom for years to come.

20

Like the Archers, those born in Sagittarius are the wanderers. And they do wander. From place to place, and sometimes from person to person. They don't want to settle, but they can make good partners if they pick independent mates. And that's a big if. Ruled by Jupiter, this mutable sign frequently lacks social graces and is known to say the wrong thing at the wrong time. You'll never tame the Archer, but if your goal is a loving state of mutual independence, you can accomplish that with a lot of freedom, a lot of latitude.

—Fearless Astrology

*S*agittarius.

The Archer.

Fire sign.

Sign of Raven-Symone, Miley Cyrus, and my own mother.

I didn't recognize Mom in my hasty read, except the love of travel, of course. The description was a much better fit with Jillian Berry, subject of my next interview.

No, Ms. Berry was not the teacher I would have chosen.

For starters, she'd given me a B minus my freshman year in beginning art. True, I had no talent for it. I'd taken her class just to see if some of my dad's creativity had trespassed into my genes. It hadn't. Berry had made that clear, and I was okay with her evaluation.

My dad could see that cosmic "it" from every angle; I couldn't. But maybe I could write my version of what people like my dad saw. While he saw images, colors, nuances, I heard and felt them.

"Hey, Logan," Berry said when I entered her classroom. "How's Mac?" The way she used my dad's nickname made me squirm.

"He's fine. Just working hard."

In every group of people, there's always one who wears too much perfume. And in the small world of our high school, Berry was that person. Her vanilla fragrance smelled like angel food cake.

Her ratty curls were overconditioned and looked as if she'd left the house before her hair was completely dry. Her famous boobs, which had shown up without covering in paintings all over town, were hidden by a gray crushed velvet jacket.

"He's such a brilliant artist. Too bad he's stuck in that advertising agency. And how's your mom?"

"Still on tour. She'll be home soon."

"Cool." She paused as if she wanted to say something else, then looked up at me. "You're going to record this interview, right?"

"No," I said.

Snider preferred that we use recorders for backup only. She thought that relying on our handwritten notes would make us stronger writers.

"Hope it won't be all messed up the way Mr. Franklin's was."

"It won't be." I sat down beside her desk. "Before we start, I need to know your birth date."

She scrunched up her lined eyes at me and said, "I'm a Sadge and proud of it. Ask away."

So she didn't want me to know the exact date. At least she seemed cool with astrology.

I tried to remember what I knew about Sagittarius. Simple stuff. Love of travel. *Check.* Far from shy. *Check.* Few social graces, translated as lack of class. *Question there.* My mom was the social grace-iest person on Earth. This teacher across from me . . . not so much.

"Ready to get started?" I asked. "This is supposed to be fun. I'll show you a list of qualities about your sign, and then you tell me if they're true or false, and why."

She nodded, toyed with her hair, and said, "Shoot."

I handed her the list.

"Travel, for sure," she said. "After I got my credential, I taught English in France and Germany."

"Great."

"The need for freedom is another one. I'm the freest person I know."

We both laughed, but I felt a little creepy. We'd barely begun, and the interview was already getting off track. At least I could use the France and Germany quote.

I reminded myself that Capricorn Snider was not about to value me if I didn't work hard on this, so I gave it another shot.

"What about your art, Ms. Berry? Is creativity a Sagittarius trait?"

"I don't know about that." She lowered her voice and flashed me a bold smile. "But I think the primitive approach I use is."

No way was I going to say the *nude* word. "You mean not painting faces? Is that a Sadge thing?"

She nodded. "A Sadge *attitude*, and I think it's a statement about love as much as anything."

Meaning that the men in her life might as well have been faceless? Nothing I wanted to think or write about.

"Maybe we could talk a little more about teaching in France and Germany," I said lamely.

She grinned again. "Poor Logan. I don't mean to rattle you. Sometimes I speak before I think."

Always, Sagittarius. "No problem," I told her.

"You seem a little uncomfortable, and I can understand why. Don't let the Gears get to you."

I straightened up in my chair. "I'm doing all right."

"Oh yeah?" She looked down at her outstretched hand and began to count it out. "One, they sabotaged your first column in the school newspaper."

"That's true," I said.

"Two, they attacked Ms. Snider's reputation."

I nodded and said, "Right again."

"Three, they threatened you at home and harmed Paige."

My pen froze on the notebook. "How do you know that?"

"I heard it from Mr. Franklin. Mr. Chiliderian saw him somewhere and mentioned it. He was worried."

"He was?"

"Oh, yes. Mr. Franklin thinks so highly of you. He's concerned."

Frankenstein? Thinks highly? Of me? Was that what she was trying to say?

"Are you sure?" I asked.

"Of course."

As I looked at her perpetual smile, I realized that Berry wasn't a bad second interview. Ms. Snider must have a sense of humor to give me this assignment. Berry was so out there that kids would love reading my astrological take on what made her the way she was. And I could do it without directly mentioning the faceless nudes.

Furthermore, this out-there art teacher had done something nice for me. She'd told me that Frankenstein cared.

"Are you all right?" she asked.

"I've had better days."

"Remember what I said, Logan. Don't be afraid of the Gears. Don't you realize that what happened proves they're the ones who are afraid of you?"

That's what Chili had said.

"It's just a little hard to believe," I told her. "Especially hard to believe after I saw the glass shatter in Chili's bedroom."

She shook her head and nailed me with her dark eyes. "Although you are looking for them, don't think they aren't keeping an eye on you. The next thing they plan won't happen if you are anywhere around."

"You're right," I said.

If I were in a better frame of mind, I would have hugged her. She'd helped me realize something I hadn't grasped on my own. I didn't need to look for the Gears. They were already looking for me.

NOTES TO SELF

Berry is so right. The Gears know that I'm going to figure out who they are and where they will strike next. But now there's a new twist, thanks to Berry. The Gears are watching me, making sure I'm not around when they do whatever they have planned for the fifteenth. New challenge. How do I make myself invisible so that I can sneak back to school and catch the Gears in the act?

A CHARACTER I'D LIKE
TO TAKE TO LUNCH

By Logan McRae

For starters, I would like to rule out Sweeney Todd and Hannibal Lecter. Literature is seldom safe, but lunch should be.

My favorite characters are in the books my mother read to me, and the best were the ones she'd saved from her own childhood. Yertle the Turtle, by Dr. Seuss, told the story of a turtle who wanted to be king of all he could see. As I snuggled against my mother and looked at the illustrations within the kelly green cover of that book, the sound of her voice became letters and words, and I felt as if I were reading, maybe even writing that story in rhyme.

At first Yertle built his empire with no problem; he just stepped on top of one shelled citizen after another. Pretty soon, he had a turtle skyscraper. But as he attempted to climb even higher, a nobody on the bottom sneezed, and you can guess what happened to Yertle and his kingdom. The nobody turtle's name was Mack, and although he didn't set out to be a hero, he brought down the king.

Since my childhood, I've read about many heroes and

villains, from Jo March to Holden Caulfield, from Desdemona to Dr. Jekyll. For this assignment, I considered choosing Zeus, who ruled Mount Olympus and was the god of sky and thunder.

I wouldn't mind asking Zeus how to throw thunder bolts at one's enemies, wouldn't mind asking how a single god managed to father everyone from Athena, Apollo, and Dionysus to Hermes, Heracles, Helen, Perseus, and the Muses. Zeus and I could connect by e-mail or telephone. That's as close as I'd want to get.

Mack's another story, an average turtle, probably as average as I am. He's my choice for a lunch date. Because I'd like to congratulate him, and because I'd like to ask him how it feels to be the one who tumbles the stack.

21

AQUARIUS WOULD RATHER THINK ABOUT A PROBLEM THAN JUMP IN HEADFIRST. BUT THERE'S A TIME TO STOP THINKING AND JUST TAKE ACTION. IF YOU ARE AN AQUARIAN TRYING TO FIND THE COURAGE TO RISK, MAKE YOUR PLAN AND THEN FOLLOW IT WITHOUT REMORSE.

—Fearless Astrology

I was ready to take action. Somehow, the book had given me what I needed—the courage, I guess—to do that. There were other changes too. I spoke up more in class. Other kids were more interested in what I had to say. At least once or twice a day, someone would ask me when I was going to expose the Gears.

We were supposed to be working on homework in Paige's room. Instead, we'd been reading *Fearless* and watching Paige fool around with some fabric. We found out that Paige had a Scorpio Moon, which explained her secretive side. Just

as we turned our attention to Trevor, my cell phone lit up
with Nathan's name.

?4u

My heart began to pound.
? I managed to text back.

miss me?

mega

He was going to ask me out again. I knew it.

hang on fri?

Yes. I mean no. Any night but Friday, the fifteenth, which
was when I had to find the Gears. I needed some time to figure out what to tell him.

not sure

bzy?

I didn't want him to think I was playing games.

more later

hurry <3

It was the first time he'd signed off with a heart.
"Just shoot me now," I said, and put down the phone.
"Nathan?" Chili asked, and Paige looked up from where

she crouched with the velvet fabric on the floor.

"He wants to get together Friday," I told them. "And you know I can't."

"What are you going to tell him?" Paige asked.

"The truth?" Chili suggested.

Such a tell-all Gemini, but maybe she was right. Perhaps it wasn't such a bad idea to let Nathan know I was trying to trap the Gears. Maybe he'd even want to come with me.

"No, that's no good," I said to them as well as myself. "What if I'm wrong? I don't want to look like a fool in front of him. Right now, if I'm wrong, no one will know except the three of us."

"You really think it will be Friday night?" Paige asked.

"There's a really good chance. Remember what I told you in San Francisco."

"Arics Moon," Chili chimed in. "Raising mischief."

"Which brings us back to Nathan," I said. "What am I going to tell him?"

"Can you say you're sick?" Paige asked.

Chili shook her head. "How would she know that she's going to be sick on Friday?"

"I meant tell him yes now and back out on Friday. A sudden flu, you could say."

"No," I said. "I'd have to fake being sick for a couple of days after, and he wouldn't want to come around me."

"That's true. What if you said you already had plans with us?"

"Paige," I said, "do you really think he'd believe that you

two wouldn't drop every possible plan in your life to give me a chance to hang out with him?"

"He might not know how close best friends are," Paige said.

"She's right," Chili said. "Couldn't you tell him that we'd planned a special night far in advance in order to celebrate Paige's birthday?" Before I could protest, she said, "And, yes, we know Paige's birthday was in March, but he doesn't. Say you don't want to hurt her feelings, but you could get together on Saturday instead."

I plopped down on the bed. "Now, that is a Gemini tall tale if I ever heard one."

"Not a lie," she said. "We do get together every birthday, and if Paige's birthday were on Friday, we would be doing that, right?"

"Right." Paige came over and sat down beside me. "Where should she say we're going, Chili?"

"I don't know. What about Java & Jazz?"

Paige's face turned bright red. "Maybe we really could go there on Friday."

"Only I'll just pretend to," I said. "Instead, I'll be at school waiting for the Gears to show up."

Which posed another problem. If the Gears were following me, how could we make them think I was with Paige and Chili?

"How are we going . . ." Chili was already ahead of me.

"Maybe we could go somewhere like the theater in the mall," I said. "We'd walk in together, and I could sneak out one of the back exits."

Paige fiddled with the amethyst around the neck of her black T-shirt. "I'd rather go to Java & Jazz, and it *is* my birthday."

"Your *fake* birthday," Chili reminded her.

"Maybe we can go there first, and then to the mall," I said.

"No, no, no." Chili shook her head so hard that her hair fell out of her ponytail. "Logan, you have to be seen with us. But it can't *be* you, get it? The Gears can only *think* they're seeing you."

"So we have to get someone to be my double?" I asked.

"Of course." Paige's voice was barely a whisper. She got up and walked across the room. "That's exactly what we're going to do."

"But who?"

Then I realized that she was staring at Calypso and smiling.

"Oh, no. You can't possibly think we can make anyone believe that this . . . this . . . dress form is human, let alone . . ." I gulped. ". . . let alone that it's me."

Without saying a word, Paige picked up my jacket from the bed and placed it around Calypso's shoulders.

"Picture this." She picked up her baseball cap and put it over the headless neck. "Pretend this is your beret. Pretend there's some curly auburn hair hanging out, hiding your face, the way it does sometimes. We could probably borrow a wig from the drama department."

Chili giggled and jumped up from the bunk bed. "This is our answer, Logan. From the waist up, we could make her your double."

I stared at the mannequin as they began tightening my jacket around it and realized that Paige was right again. Calypso could be me. Maybe. If no one got too close.

NOTES TO SELF

The next day I approached Snider about letting me give away weekly astrology readings, without mentioning our hidden agenda. In her calm, elegant way, she agreed, saying it would be fun and draw attention to my column. "I wouldn't be surprised if it helped us win another award," she said. "Three years in a row, Logan. Wouldn't that be great?"

Everything is going my way. Now I just need to catch the Gears on Friday. If they are following me, they'll think I'm out with Chili and Paige, especially if they see us at the coffee shop earlier. They won't know that I'm really at school waiting for them with my camera phone. Can I pull it off? Can I show up at Java & Jazz with my friends, get in the car, change places with Calypso, and then make the Gears think my double is really me? I've got to try.

22

A NEW MOON IN ARIES SIGNALS SHORT TEMPERS AND RISK-TAKING. CERTAIN SIGNS, ESPECIALLY ARIES, WILL BE MORE AFFECTED THAN OTHERS. REGARDLESS OF YOUR SUN SIGN, BE READY FOR IMPULSIVE ACTIONS AND EMOTIONAL REACTIONS. PREPARE FOR THE NEW MOON IN ARIES, BY ALL MEANS, BUT DO NOT FEAR IT.

—*Fearless Astrology*

y Thursday I was ready for the Gears. Tomorrow night would be the new moon. In Aries. I knew we were already feeling the effects of it and was ready to take some risks. If I had my way, the Gears would be the ones experiencing some emotional reactions when they found themselves exposed.

Soon I'd know if I was one of the Monterey finalists. Frankenstein had been his version of nice to me since the night the Gears called my cell and broke Chili's window. I even got an A minus on my lunch-with-a-character essay.

"Better," he said when he handed the paper back to me that day. "At first, I thought using a kids book was a cop-out, but you made it work."

"I tried," I said. "I—"

"If you're serious about Monterey, you're going to have to hit the ground running."

What was that jock metaphor supposed to mean? "I am serious," I said. "I want it more than anything."

"Why?"

"What?"

He took off his glasses and looked into my eyes. "Why do you want to go to Monterey this summer, McRae?"

"Because . . ." I couldn't find the words. My mouth went dry. "Well, because I want to write, and I know I'll be able to if I can get that fellowship."

"What will it give you that you don't have here?" he asked.

"Real writers," I said. "The guest speakers have published newspaper and magazine articles, as well as books. And the other kids, well, they're probably interested in the same things I am."

"So you want to go so that you can learn from published writers and meet students with interests similar to your own?"

I felt as if I was taking some kind of quiz, and I probably was.

"More than that," I said. "I want . . ."

The sound of voices in the back of the room rescued me from having to say more.

"Why don't you try writing about it?" Frankenstein said. Then, in a lower voice, he added, "That's not an assignment, McRae, just a suggestion."

For some reason, I gushed, "Thank you."

As I rushed out of the classroom, I saw Nathan with the two giants, Jared and J.T., talking by the water fountain. Nathan leaned against the wall as if waiting for me. Nathan waiting for me? Now that would be cool.

I stopped and looked back.

Nathan left his friends and walked over to me.

"Hey," he said.

How could any guy this perfect light up when he saw me?

"Hi, Nathan."

"Come with me." He touched my elbow and guided me down the hall. "Let's sit in my car for a minute. I've got something to ask you."

Could this really be happening? Could Nathan be touching me in public for all, including Geneva, to see? Even if that touching was only on the sleeve of my jacket? Even if Geneva didn't happen to pass by?

I had to remind myself to be cool, to keep breathing evenly.

"Need to talk to you," he said.

"Sure."

I let him urge me around a corner, into the parking lot and the black Honda. So I might be late to Spanish. Mr. Macias was cool. I could probably get away with it.

Nathan climbed in the driver's side. "Now," he said.

"Finally."

I looked up at him, my heart pounding. "What?"

"I don't mean to come off like a creep," he said, "but I just have to know. Why can't you see me tomorrow night?"

So that was it.

"I told you. It's a birthday dinner for Paige."

"Isn't it a little late for that?" His blue eyes narrowed, and I knew somehow he'd figured out that I lied to him. "Birth dates are printed in the school newspaper, you know."

"And you remembered Paige's?"

"No." Now he was the one with the flushed face. "I looked it up in the online archives."

Looked it up? For me? I mattered that much?

"You thought I lied to you?" I attempted to sound shocked as I tried desperately to think of another lie to convince him that he was wrong about the first one.

"Your text message sounded different," he said. "So, I decided to check it out and found out that her birthday was in March."

"We didn't have a chance to celebrate when we should have. Chili and I promised Paige we'd do it tomorrow."

He seemed to relax. "And you aren't making up all of this so that you can go out with some other guy?"

"Of course not," I said.

"Logan, do you know how much I want to see you tomorrow?"

He was close enough to kiss and didn't seem to care. I didn't either. Could I possibly have a boyfriend?

"I want to see you too," I said. "But I can't desert my friends."

"You're a loyal person. That's part of what I like about you." He squeezed my hand again. "Just tell me when I can see you."

"I already told you," I said. "Saturday works for me if it works for you."

"Cool."

And right there, in what my gram would call broad daylight, he kissed the rest of whatever I was going to say right off my face.

"Nathan," I gasped when he finally let go of me. "We'll both be expelled if anyone sees us."

He grinned and ran his fingers along my neck. I shivered.

"It would be worth it," he said, "to get kicked out for kissing you."

NOTES TO SELF

I'm curled up here in bed trying to keep from thinking about Nathan's lips while I write an answer to Frankenstein's question. Why is the summer fellowship so important to me? I'm glad it's not an assignment because there's no way I'd be able to figure out the reason if I thought he or anyone else was going to read what I wrote. I want the fellowship because although I suck at art and golf, I write pretty well. Not that it's easy for me. It's not. As far as I can figure, the most difficult part of writing is the thinking. The rest is just getting it down. So I guess I want the fellowship because, until I found the book, I felt as if I didn't belong in this school, this city, and once in a while, even in my own house. I want the fellowship to show that I'm good enough to get it, that I do belong somewhere. Wow. I said it. Hope you're happy, Frankenstein, wherever you are. Is that what you've been trying to pull out of me?

23

NEW MOONS OCCUR WHEN THE MOON IS BETWEEN THE EARTH AND THE SUN AND IS INVISIBLE. ALSO KNOWN AS THE DARK MOON, EACH ONE OFFERS DIFFERENT POSSIBILITIES AND CHALLENGES. LEARNING THE RHYTHMS OF THE MOON IS LIKE LEARNING TO SWIM IN THE SEA OF LIFE. THE SOONER YOU LEARN HOW, THE MORE NATURAL IT WILL FEEL.

—Fearless Astrology

t was time. Friday night. The new moon was here, and it was a good time for undercover work. The three of us put on our zodiac-friendly gemstones, and Calypso wore my gray beret and rust-colored scarf. I had to admit it looked better wrapped around her unrealistic 36-20-38 flexible form than it had around the real me.

Chili and Paige were dressed in jeans and cute tops. Chili's was chocolate-brown cashmere with a V neck that showed off her matching tourmaline. Paige's, a fluttery retro empire top of pink, turquoise, purple, and black, barely covered her slender belly.

"Look at you," I said.

Paige blushed, then tapped the amethyst on her chest.

"Is that a Pucci top?" Chili asked.

"Only the fabric. I designed the pattern and made it myself."

"You did? I should have known."

Paige nodded and blinked behind her glasses. "It was actually pretty easy."

"Look out, Hunter," Chili said.

"I'm sure glad we're celebrating my birthday there this time. Even though it's not my birthday."

I was wearing black top to bottom. Turtleneck. Jacket. Jeans. The plan was to show up at Java & Jazz and hang out. Then I would send Paige, Chili, and Calypso off to a drive-through fast-food place. It was the only way we could keep anyone from realizing that one of the three of us—I mean, them—wasn't a real person.

I put on the hat and scarf, we stuffed Calypso into the back-seat, and walked into the coffee place, making sure everyone noticed us, knowing the Gears were watching. I glanced to the front where Hunter usually stood. He wasn't there.

"Just my luck," Paige said.

"Let's ask," I suggested.

"Please don't. He'll know I like him."

"Well, he has to find out at some point," Chili whispered.

"Hi," she said to the new cute-but-clueless guy behind the counter. "Where's Hunter?"

"Hunter who?" he asked.

So much for that. Whether Hunter quit, was fired, or simply had a day off was not our problem now. I'd been seen in Java & Jazz. We could all quietly leave and let Calypso take my place after they dropped me off at school.

Chili wasn't satisfied.

"Hunter," she repeated, and ran her hand along her arm as if pointing out imaginary tattoos.

"Oh, that dude." He turned to the guy on the other side of the partition. "Where's Hunter, the guy with the tats?"

"Out sick." He grinned at us. "Sorry, girls. Shall I tell him you dropped by?"

"We'll check back," Chili said.

"Time to go," I whispered.

Paige nearly knocked me down. "Let's get out of here," she muttered.

We got out, propped up Calypso, and put my beret and scarf on her. Then we drove around, with me ducked down in the backseat, just in case Gear members were still behind us.

"They won't be," Chili said. "Once they saw us at J&J, you know they took off."

We drove around the school once. Paige looked behind us on the two-way street.

"Is everything okay?" I asked her.

"No one's following us."

"Are you sure you're going to be all right?" Chili demanded. "If something happens before we get back, call me."

"If I need to, I will. And you can't stick around. They'll recognize your car for sure."

"All right, then," Chili said. "We'll be back in an hour. You can get up now. No one can see you."

She pulled into the far corner of the school parking lot, far away from the few remaining cars. We stayed in the shadows.

"See you later," I said.

I opened the car door and got out.

My first thought was that I wished I had the scarf I'd wrapped around Calypso's skinny neck. The almost deserted parking lot was so eerie and silent that I wanted to chase down Chili and tell her I had changed my mind. Her car was creeping through the lot so slowly that I could have caught up with it and jumped back inside. Instead, I watched it coast away from me. I'd have to do this one by myself.

I stared up into the darkened sky, knowing that the Aries new moon was hiding as I was. *Where do I start?* I wondered again.

My skin tingled, and not just from the weather. I felt something was already happening here—or soon would be.

Although the corridors were lit at each end, I could hide by pressing myself up against the lockers and blending into the shadows. Regardless of how cold it was, I knew I could stick it out. One hour, Gears or no Gears.

Slowly, I made my way along the lockers, which were more

frozen than I was. Something rustled in the trees. I shuddered. Stopped. Just the wind.

Misty light illuminated the corner I would have to turn in order to get to the administration office. That's where the Gears had attacked before, and if they were the creatures of habit I believed they were, they'd attack again.

I got there, took a deep breath, and with my sleeve hiding my face, dashed around that corner. *Whew*. The administration office was only a hundred feet away.

Just then, I heard laughter. Male laughter. I'd found the Gears! No wonder they hadn't followed Chili's car. They'd gotten here ahead of me.

"Here's the paint," somebody said.

I yanked open my bag, pulled out my camera phone, and clicked it on.

"Quiet," said a muffled voice. "Give me the flashlight."

They were a blur, like players on a football field. I had to get closer and moved down the hall along the lockers, hoping they were too busy to notice a small dark shape.

I had them.

Just then, someone yelled, "Shit. Look over there."

A bright light washed over me. I tried to escape it, but I was totally out in the open. It blinded me, forced me to close my eyes. I put my hands to my face and tried to peer between my fingers.

Hazy shapes darted in front of me.

"Run!" a gruff voice shouted.

I couldn't see them, but maybe my camera could. Heart pounding, I pointed it at the blur and snapped.

"What the hell?" Another male voice boomed from down the hall. "McRae, what is going on here?"

Frankenstein.

I rushed toward his voice.

"Are you okay?" He looked so angry that I was almost afraid to talk.

"The Gears," I managed to get out, and pointed. "Let's go after them."

"You wait here. I mean it."

He took off running, and I tried to catch my breath. I had been right about the Gears, right about tonight. If only Frankenstein could catch up with them.

He returned shortly. I took one look at his scowl and knew that he hadn't had any luck.

"Come on," he said. "I'll wait with you in teacher parking until someone comes to take you home."

"Chili and Paige are supposed to pick me up," I told him. "As soon as I call them, they'll be here."

"I'm not leaving until they are."

"What were you doing here so late?" I asked as we crossed the parking lot.

"Drama."

He took the cover off his car. It was as, well, *yellow* as ever.

The moment I looked inside, however, I knew this vehicle was special. The white leather upholstery looked and smelled brand-new.

He seemed to be waiting for me to comment, so I said, "Cool car, Mr. Franklin."

Yet this wasn't just a perfect car. It was a lonely one. I got the distinct feeling that he was the only person who had ever sat in it. Poor Frankenstein.

"Tuck-and-roll upholstery," he said, catching me eyeing it. "Now, tell me how you knew these idiots were coming back here."

"You wouldn't believe me."

"You mean the astrology stuff?"

I nodded and turned back toward him. "There's a way to figure out dangerous days. This is one of them."

I stopped short of saying there'd be another one in less than two weeks.

"Those punks will be back again. You know that."

"I'll get them next time."

"Not without me." He stood next to the open driver's door and said, "Logan, I'm not suggesting that I believe what you're doing is at all sensible, but I don't want you to do it by yourself. Next time, talk to me, will you? Don't try to do it alone."

It was the first time he'd offered to help.

The first time he'd ever called me Logan.

"All right," I said, and looked at my watch. Chili would be here any moment. I hadn't identified the Gears, but I had gotten Frankenstein more on my side. I could almost feel his loneliness.

"What is it?" he demanded, as if knowing I was thinking about him.

"Well," I said, "I've been looking at some astrological profiles, and although I'm no expert, I think that you might be happier if you showed your soft side a little more often."

His laugh was harsh. "Thanks for the tip. I'll remember it the next time I'm chasing a bunch of punks in the middle of the night."

"I'm serious, Mr. Franklin." I winced as I heard myself say his name correctly. Thank goodness I hadn't called him *Frankenstein*. "I know you have feelings for a certain person, and Taurus-Capricorn is a good match astrologically."

"What are you talking about?" His eyes narrowed, but I went ahead anyway.

"All I'm trying to say is that the softer side of Taurus can appeal to a Capricorn. They are hard workers and it can be difficult for them to let down their guards."

I stared back at him and felt as miserable as this car of his must feel. Why had I—a student who desperately needed his approval and respect—even dared to bring up the subject of his love life? It sure wasn't getting me any closer to going to Monterey. But that's not why I brought it up. I really wanted to help Frankenstein. How crazy was that?

"Well, McRae," he finally said, "I'll give that some thought."

Back to my last name again. I deserved it. Yet he didn't seem angry.

"I can tell you more when I do your chart," I said.

"My chart? What are you talking about?"

"You heard about the free charts the journalism department is giving away, right?"

He nodded. "Right."

"Well, you're this week's winner," I said.

"That's impossible. I didn't even enter."

"I guess someone must have entered for you."

"That's it," he said. "I've had enough craziness for one night. Here comes your ride."

I turned my head to see the Spyder heading toward us. As they got closer, I could make out Paige's and Chili's shocked expressions. In the backseat, Calypso still wore my hat, the auburn wig draped in front of what would have been her face.

"What the . . . ?" Frankenstein squinted and stared at the car.

"See you Monday," I said, and ran toward them before he could ask any more questions.

NOTES TO SELF

I think Frankenstein likes me a little. He'll have to tell Dr. West, the vice principal, what happened. Hope I don't get called in. Chili and Paige were speechless when I told them I'd almost caught the Gears. Well, make that momentarily speechless. After the initial shock, they bombarded me with questions about what the Gears were doing and how many of them were there. I didn't have any answers. The darkness provided by the new moon had hidden the Gears too. But I was right about the date, and I'll be right about the twenty-fifth too.

24

THE TAURUS/AQUARIUS FRIENDSHIP IS NOT IMPOSSIBLE.
FIXED EARTH AND FIXED AIR WON'T WIN ANY AWARDS FOR
FLEXIBILITY, BUT BOTH ARE USUALLY SLOW TO ANGER.
EVEN WHEN THESE TWO DISAGREE, THERE IS LITTLE
BLOODSHED AND FEW SCARS—EXTERNALLY, AT LEAST.

—*Fearless Astrology*

Taurus/Aquarius. That was Frankenstein and me.
"Not impossible" was not exactly what I was
hoping for, but at least we could communicate. I was
starting to see that more and more. It was probably
not a good idea to say what I did to him the other night
about Snider.

The fellowship finalists were supposed to be announced
this week. That meant Frankenstein had to know today. I was
determined to get to his room early. Dina and Kat were coming toward me, wearing their usual smirks. Kat looked

through me, and Dina broke into a smile.

"Hiiii, Logan," she sang out.

I nodded and hurried down the hall.

When I got to Frankenstein's room, I was surprised to see Geneva just leaving.

"Hey, Logan. Congratulations," she said. "Um, I hear you *almost* caught the Gears."

"Where'd you hear that?" I couldn't miss the way she emphasized *almost*.

"Everyone's talking about it. Good for you and, hey, I want to win one of those charts of yours."

"It's a weekly drawing," I said.

"So draw my name." She pushed a chunk of hair behind one ear, and I couldn't help thinking that she looked like a self-satisfied Siamese cat. "You know, I'm really glad I decided to go with your column. We could take best school newspaper for the third year in a row."

We meaning *she*.

"Right."

On that happy note, she said, "See you," and took off down the hall. Finally, I might have a minute to ask Frankenstein to tell me if they'd selected the fellowship finalists.

He was standing by the door, watching us. His short-sleeved polo shirt was as boldly yellow as his Corvette. Not his best color, but I guess he hadn't figured that out yet.

I ran up to him and blurted, "Do you have a moment to talk?"

"Of course." A smile lit his broad face. "You want to hear

about my so-called sign, right? I decided to be a good sport."

Taurus a good sport? Yes, the Bull did like peace, as long as it was on his terms. But what was he talking about? Was he going to tell me the finalists or not?

"Meaning?" I asked.

His eyes sparkled, and I realized just then that he wasn't wearing his glasses. "Meaning that if you stick around after class, I'll give you the information so that you can do my chart. The year, time, place—everything."

"Well, great," I said. "Thank you."

"I also want to talk to you about something else," he said.

The fellowship. That's all it could be.

Chili walked in just then and flashed him a fake-friendly smile. She'd been that way, even laughing at his lame jokes in class, ever since she decided that "we" liked him now.

I took my place beside her.

"Everyone knows you almost caught the Gears," she whispered.

There was that word again.

"Everyone including Geneva," I said.

"No. You're a hero, Logan. I can't tell you how many kids have asked me how they can get you to do their charts. Snider says the list for the drawing is huge."

"I already *drew* this week's winner, if you know what I mean," I whispered. "And he happens to be standing in front of us."

"Chiliderian? McRae?" Frankenstein shouted. "Are you

ladies ready to begin?"

Whispers buzzed around the room. Talking about me, I knew. Chili giggled. I met Frankenstein's eyes and nodded. I'd have to stay after in order to learn if he'd picked the three finalists yet. How was I going to wait that long?

Maybe it was my imagination, but he didn't seem as mean in class as he used to. Not once did he attack Charles Bellamy, who'd changed seats and now sat one empty desk away from me.

After class, several kids came up to me, asking questions about their signs. All I wanted was time alone with Frankenstein. I told people we could talk later. They seemed all right with that, as if I was some kind of star.

"McRae!"

Frankenstein's demanding coach voice was more effective than the bell, and just as jarring. Kids tripped over one another getting away from me and scrambling out the door. Poor Charles was nearly trampled.

Once they left, Frankenstein got up, sat on the edge of his desk, and handed me an index card, where he had printed the information about his date and place of birth. One down. Hunter and one more lucky winner to go.

"Thanks," I said, and waited for the rest. "Is there anything else?" *Please tell me*, I begged. I already knew what it was, and could tell from his expression that I was in trouble.

He nodded. "The real reason I asked you to stay after class is that I wanted to let you know that, according to schedule, we're down to three finalists for the Monterey fellowship."

My knees buckled. "Oh," I managed to say.

He tapped the folder on his desk. "You're one of them."

I wanted to cry, wanted to hug him.

"Thank you for telling me." My voice was a dry squawk.

"All three finalists will be announced later today," he said. "One of them is Charles Bellamy. He has natural talent and a good story, but only if he's able to tell it."

Charles? My competition? Before I could decide how I felt about that, I blurted out the truth.

"He sure does. It's a great story."

Frankenstein drew back. "You know about Bellamy?"

"His dad being Charlie Bell, you mean? Yeah, Charles told me."

"I wouldn't have guessed that." He seemed to approve, though.

Maybe Charles would get extra points for telling me who his dad was. Maybe that was part of the *digging deep* Frankenstein was constantly telling me I needed to do.

Just then, the door opened, and Dr. West, the vice principal, came inside the classroom. He looked shorter, balder, and meaner than ever.

"Can we step outside?" he asked Frankenstein. From the look he gave me, I knew it was about what had happened Friday night.

Not now. Not when I finally had a moment to talk to my teacher alone. Please let Frankenstein tell him no, that he couldn't leave before we finished our conversation.

"Be right back," Frankenstein told me.

So, there we were, just the folder on his desk and me. All I had to do was reach out and flip it open. My hand was trembling.

Just as I reached out, the door opened, and Frankenstein returned.

"Sorry," he said, then looked at the folder and back to me. "McRae, you wouldn't."

"I didn't," I said. "Honest."

"I'm going to give you the benefit of the doubt." He slid back into his chair. "Now, where was I?"

"Charles," I told him. "And one other finalist."

He cleared his throat and said, "Geneva Hamilton."

My head felt light. It was all I could do to keep from bursting into tears.

"But she's a senior."

He nodded, and I realized that his eyes were much kinder without his glasses.

"But she's two months shy of eighteen. That's the cutoff age. Besides, she's going to major in journalism."

Great. So Geneva not only wanted Nathan—she also wanted my dream.

"What happens next?" I was surprised how calm and even my voice sounded, although I was screaming inside.

"You have until the end of May to submit your writing sample. Your last essay was a good start, but it has to be better. Each of us on the committee will have equal input."

"Who are the committee members?" I asked.

"I guess there's no reason to keep it secret," he said. "Dr. West, Mr. Macias, Ms. Snider, and me."

So these were the ones who'd be evaluating my writing skills for the people at Monterey. How would they rate me? I knew Mr. Macias liked me. He'd given me an A in Spanish last year. Dr. West seemed indifferent to all of us. Snider was clearly impressed by Geneva. And Frankenstein?

Taurus, I reminded myself. *Fixed but fair.*

"So what will it take to win?" I asked.

"Voice." He lowered his own, even though we were the only people in the room.

"What do you mean?"

He stood up and started pacing. I wondered if it was because he was no longer comfortable looking into my eyes.

"It's who you are, McRae. You can't invent your voice. It's all you have as a writer. And you already have it, a sum of all your experiences writing, reading, winning, and losing." He stretched as if trying to remove a heavy weight from his shoulders. "You do understand that the person who represents this school for the Monterey fellowship must have a strong voice and must dig deeply into his or her emotions?"

The way an award-winning school newspaper editor, who just happened to be exude confidence and poise, could do.

I managed to nod and say, "Yes, I understand."

And I left the room wanting to throw up.

NOTES TO SELF

I'm pretty sure how the Monterey thing is going to be resolved, and it makes me want to bawl my eyes out. I might if I weren't wearing that new Redhead Perfection mascara Chili bought for me. Auburn trails down my cheeks won't win me any points from Frankenstein (or Nathan). Geneva, the lying Libra, can probably "dig deep." All right, make that *deeply*. Bottom line, why can't I? I don't know. But I will figure it out. First I am going to study her chart top to bottom. Maybe it's not as perfect as she is top to bottom. And maybe, as my gram always says, pigs can fly.

25

STUDYING THE CHART OF A LIBRA MAY LEAD YOU TO BE AS INCONCLUSIVE AS THE SIGN ITSELF. HOW, YOU MAY ASK, CAN THIS BEAUTY-LOVING, CHARMING, RULED-BY-VENUS PERSON BE ANYTHING BUT WONDERFUL, RIGHT? WRONG. LIBRA'S ENVIOUS, COMPETITIVE SIDE HAS -LITTLE IN COMMON WITH THAT EVER LOVELY, PLACID SURFACE. IF YOU ARE COMPETING WITH A LIBRA FOR ANYTHING FROM A JOB TO A PARKING SPACE, DON'T GIVE UP. TRUE, THIS SIGN'S ENVIOUS NATURE COULD MEAN A FIGHT TO THE FINISH. BUT IT COULD ALSO BE THAT THE OFTEN FICKLE LIBRA WILL FOCUS ALL OF THAT POWER SOMEWHERE ELSE. FOR NOW.

—Fearless Astrology

I felt so low the next day that not even the not-so-glowing description of Libra could improve my mood. It must be the sign of every beautiful, successful person on earth. Libra was cardinal air. Cardinal, meaning one of the take-charge signs. Air, meaning the initiator of relationships. Meaning that Geneva would lead the way to any battle she wanted to win.

But why did she want the fellowship? Was it before or after she'd decided she wanted Nathan? This was her senior year. Why spend her last summer in Monterey? Maybe she was just going for the fellowship to prove she could get it. Ironic that once I was starting to win Frankenstein over, Geneva, who hadn't bothered to try winning over anybody, would probably win.

"I thought you were going to study Geneva's chart," Chili said.

We were at Java & Jazz, hoping, for the sake of Paige and her flax-colored shaggy knit top, that Hunter was working. So far, we hadn't spotted him.

"Already did," I said. "She has Libra in three places, and some critical Virgo too. I might as well give up."

"Logan." Paige grabbed my wrist across the table so hard that her oversize ring cut into my hand. "You can't let that little vixen win. Did you find out anything new about her?"

"Other than she's aggressive, judgmental, and gets her way?" I asked. "Not really. Except that Libra has a hard time committing, of course. It's A today, B tomorrow, and XYZ by the weekend."

"Then maybe she won't make time to write a decent essay," Paige said.

"Let's hope so."

"And you have something she doesn't," Chili added. "You have astrology."

I felt like crying. I might not have the life I would have picked, but I was beyond lucky in the friends department.

"Do you realize," I said, "how rare it is for three girls as different as we are to be this close?"

"We trust one another," Chili said. "We know one another's secrets. How many girls at our school can you say that about?"

None, I thought. Put Geneva and Kat on the top of that non-list.

"None," Paige said, as if she could read my mind. "Oh, look."

Hunter appeared behind the counter. No more blue hair. He'd shaved it all off. He still had the tats, though. His dark eyes didn't leave Paige's face.

Chili jerked around and nearly spilled another cup of coffee. Good thing Mercury wasn't in retrograde the way it had been the last time we were here, or she'd be wearing her latte all over that white shirt.

"I admit it, Paige," she whispered. "He's hot."

Just then, the door opened, and in walked Trevor and Nathan. My mouth went dry. Had they known we'd be here? They headed over to us, and Nathan dragged a small round table close to ours.

"Hey," Trevor said and pulled his chair next to Chili's.

"What's up?" Her tone was so friendly and casual that I almost believed this was something we did every day.

I looked at Nathan's eyes. They were glowing. I hoped he could tell I was happy to see him, but not so happy that I seemed desperate.

"Hey, Nathan."

Cute boy. Cute boy. That's all I could think at that moment.

"I got it," he said, and sat down beside me. "I got the part. You were right, Logan. You're magic."

"You deserved it," I told him. "I've been saying that all along. By the way, I found out I'm one of the Monterey finalists."

"Cool. Who are the others?"

"Charles Bellamy and Geneva Hamilton," I said in a calm voice.

"Really?" He looked surprised, but I wasn't sure if it was because of Charles or Geneva. "Well, congratulations."

"Thanks."

He glanced down at my coffee cup. "Want a refill?"

"I'm fine."

"Let me get something, and let's walk around the mall, okay?"

"Sure," I managed to reply, and he headed for the counter. I looked over at Chili. "We're going to . . ." I was so flustered that I couldn't finish the sentence.

"Great." She broke into a grin. "Have fun."

Once we were outside, we stood in front of the coffee shop.

Stores stretched in both directions along the faux cobbled path.

"So," Nathan said. "Which way do you want to go?"

"I don't care." How true that was. I was happy to be with him. "I'm glad you got the part."

"Me too." He started walking in the direction of the Cheesecake Factory, the largest building on the mall. "Frankenstein hasn't seemed as grouchy as usual. Have you had anything to do with that?"

"I don't think so. His Sun sign, as you know if you read my column, is Taurus."

"There's not a kid in school who didn't read your column." He nudged me with an elbow. "They're calling you Astro Girl."

I tried to ignore the heat flooding my cheeks. "Well, a Taurus is generally fair and not mean-spirited. He did the right thing by giving you the part."

"Logan, could I ask you something?" He stopped and looked at me, his expression serious.

"Sure. What?"

"Would you do *my* chart?" He looked down at his coffee as if he were embarrassed. "I'm not asking you to cheat and let me win the drawing or anything. There are some things I need to figure out."

"Like what?"

"Not about you and me. Some family stuff." He seemed to hesitate. "Will you do it?"

You and me. As if we were a unit.

"Sure," I finally said. "I'll do it when I get home tonight, if you want."

"I knew I could count on you." He gave me a quick kiss. "I don't want to take a lot of your time. Write your essay first."

"It won't take that much time," I said.

Not with all the research I'd already done in advance.

NOTES TO SELF

I wonder why it's so important to Nathan to have me do his chart. He said it isn't about us, but that's the first thing I'm concentrating on, of course. His Venus is in Aquarius. My sign, so that must be good, right? No, turns out that a male with his Venus in Aquarius wants a partner who can keep him guessing, someone quirky enough to keep him wondering. Not even close to me, but then let me see what I can do about that. But first I need to write a brand new essay that will be good enough to submit for my writing sample.

26

Mars is the warrior god, although his energy is felt in women as well as men. Wherever you find Mars, you'll also find aggression and selfishness. In water signs (Cancer, Scorpio, Pisces), Mars boils. In earth signs (Taurus, Virgo, Capricorn), he's stubborn. In air signs (Gemini, Libra, Aquarius), he argues, and in fire signs (Aries, Leo, Sagittarius), he escalates the passion. Discovering the placement of Mars is essential. It shows us the way in which even the meekest person expresses aggression.

—Fearless Astrology

loved what I was learning about Mars. Mine was in Gemini, which meant I expressed my aggression with words. Now if I could just write them down. With a Mars in Sagittarius, Nathan might have a tendency toward bluntness, with a free, adventurous spirit that craved independence. His ideal love match would be someone— me, I hoped—with a good sense of humor, who liked to have fun, and did not press for commitment. I'd have to remember that when we met before class to go over his chart.

The next morning Chili and Paige were grinning like twin Cheshires, as my gram would say. Paige seemed more confident, and looked it in her oversize glasses with her hair falling free around her face. Chili seemed less scattered. We were changing, all of us, right before my eyes. All we could talk about was the night before.

"That book has transformed our lives, Logan," Paige said, and I remembered the line on the cover and how I'd felt the first time I read it. *Transform your life . . .*

"It's amazing," I agreed.

"You know that Trevor and Nathan showed up at the coffee shop looking for you and Chili. And Hunter . . ."

"Yes, you actually managed to speak to the tattooed man this time," I said. "Talk about change."

"Well, let's just hope the book keeps doing its magic." With a shake of her fabulously highlighted hair, Chili opened the door.

Nathan was waiting for me in the parking lot, just as we'd planned. He grinned when he saw me, and my heart beat faster. *Transformed* was the right word, for sure. I didn't have to fake feeling confident anymore. I just was.

"See you later." Chili grinned, and she and Paige began walking toward the main hallway.

"Did you finish it?" Nathan asked as we followed them.

"I did. You have a great chart, Nathan."

"I do?"

I nodded. "Very cool. A fun-loving personality. Acting is a natural for you."

"Now, if only I could convince my mom." He made a face.

"Do it in a playful way," I said. "If you're too blunt, it could make her defensive."

Before he could answer, Kat caught up with us. As usual, she was wearing her gold-and-navy cheerleader uniform.

"Hey, Nathan," she said, but I was the one she was looking at. "I want one of those free horoscopes." Her smile was as fake and as friendly as if she'd never had the meltdown in the school restroom.

"Did you sign up with Ms. Snider?"

"Oh, yeah." She tossed her short dark hair. "I just wanted to make sure you knew that I really want it."

"You made that pretty clear the other day," I said.

"Oh, *that*." More shrugs and tossing of hair. She glanced at Nathan as if he were part of this too. "Trevor and I had a misunderstanding is all, and I was dealing with a lot of stress. It's okay now, though. The four of us will have to go out sometime."

The four of us. It's a good thing Aquarius is not a violent sign, or my fingers would have been around that skinny Aries throat.

"We need to get to class," I muttered.

"See you." Kat's eyes met mine. "Just remember what I said about the chart. I really want it."

We watched her walk away, and then finally Nathan said, "Can you believe that?"

"She offered me her jacket and Coach bag if I'd figure out her chart," I told him. "Then she threw a fit in the restroom when I turned her down."

"Crazy." He shook his head. "Jared dated her in junior high and said she was nuts then."

Had Geneva's younger brother been interested in Kat before or after he'd been interested in me?

"When was that?" I asked.

"Seventh grade," I think. "Kat went to private school. They were together that summer and fall."

The same summer and fall I'd thought Jared liked me. The same time we'd kissed.

"Well, she claims she's back with Trevor now," I said.

"She's not. I know that for a fact."

Thank goodness, I thought. "Really?"

"Yeah." He reached out and took my hand as we walked. I couldn't believe the warmth of it.

"So Kat was lying?" I asked.

"She sure was. Trevor likes someone else, as I'm sure you know. But that's all I can say. After what happened with Kat, he's going to take his time. Doesn't want to deal with a bunch of gossip."

So Scorpio of Trevor.

"I wouldn't tell anyone," I said. Except Chili. And Paige, of course.

"No can do."

I looked in his eyes and knew he meant it. Smart of him too.

"That's okay," I said. "It's good that you can keep a secret."

He squeezed my hand again. "Now, can we go talk about my chart?"

Sure thing, Leo.

I reminded myself to be fun-loving and flashed him a smile.

"Absolutely," I said.

NOTES TO SELF

Nathan was engrossed by all of the information I'd found in the book. I made sure to describe his traits in positive terms. I could tell by his questions that he's really aggressive about topics his mom doesn't want to hear. When I explained, in the most upbeat way possible, the significance of Mars in Sagittarius, he said he was going to try to be less blunt with her. And then, his eyes gleaming with adoration—probably for himself, but maybe for me too—he told me I was the smartest girl he knew. I remember that Venus in Aquarius of his, and know not to get all gushy and possessive. It won't be easy, though. I'm really starting to like him.

27

Trines are astrological ties that can bind. You'll find special compatibility and understanding with someone who is trined to your Sun. Sun signs are trined based on their elements. Fire signs (Aries, Leo, Sagittarius); earth signs (Taurus, Virgo, Capricorn); air signs (Gemini, Libra, Aquarius); water signs (Cancer, Pisces, Scorpio). The trine of 120 degrees can bring a feeling of instant rapport and usually results in a harmonious relationship.

—Fearless Astrology

s earth signs, Frankenstein and Snider were trined. That meant that regardless of how different they appeared on the surface, they

could have—what were the terms? —yes, that's right: *instant rapport* and a *harmonious relationship*.

They had to be a match, right? If *he* could be more flexible and if *she* could be less focused on work. On second thought, why should anyone be *less* of what they were meant to be? If the trine aspect was working, maybe none of their differences mattered. I hoped that was the case. They were cute together. And they could be compatible. Just like Nathan and me. Tonight I'd be with him again.

It wasn't my imagination. Kids were treating me differently, and I was liking it. Seniors who'd walked right past me before stopped and asked about their signs. I quickly figured out something positive to say. If the person was a Libra, I'd use words like "fair," instead of "wishy-washy." If it was an Aries, I'd mention "leadership" and not the tendency to leave jobs unfinished.

"You're like Miss Popular these days," Chili said as we drove to Java & Jazz to give Paige her thrill for the night.

"You really think so?"

"Everybody's so into you," Paige said. "They look up to you, Logan."

After we left Java & Jazz, Chili was going to drop me at the drama classroom. Unfortunately, Hunter was "out sick" again, according to the smirking guy we'd talked to the first time we'd stalked Hunter there.

"An Aries can be unreliable," I said as we walked back to the car. "I'm not so sure about him, Paige."

"Signs can't be all bad or all good," she said. "Haven't you said that about a hundred times?"

"True," I conceded. "Even though Hunter likes to stand out with his tats and hair, you don't see him throwing fits like Kat. And they're both the same Sun sign."

Still, the ephemeris had warned about a period of strife. An Aries thrown into the mix could be like tossing a match into gasoline.

As we climbed into the car, I felt a chill. *No*, I thought, *don't say a word. There's no reason to suspect that Hunter is one of the Gears.*

Then I remembered our lame attempt to catch them. Hunter hadn't been at work that night either. Could he have been one of the boys I'd heard?

"Why so quiet?" Paige asked from the backseat, as if she could hear me thinking.

"Just getting ready for Nathan." Far from a lie. I reached for my tube of lip gloss.

Chili squealed, and I nearly glossed my nose.

"Paige, look."

Sure enough, there was Hunter hanging out in the parking lot, talking to Trevor, both of them in jackets. They looked up and nodded when we drove in. What was this junior college guy doing in our high school parking lot with the senior guy? Especially when the junior college guy was supposed to be "off sick" from work?

Paige waved a little more enthusiastically than we might

have advised.

"There's our evening," Chili said. "I'm so glad I decided to drive you here."

"Did you tell Trevor you were going to?" I asked.

"Of course." She grinned. "You have fun."

Nathan came out of the classroom and started toward me. I tried to look back and say good-bye to Chili and Paige, but Chili's car was heading back toward the boys.

"Hey." Nathan hugged me out there in view of anyone who might be looking. "Missed you."

He no longer seemed down. In fact, he seemed more interested in me than ever. Why was that? Because I was keeping him guessing the way the book suggested? Or was he attracted by my sudden fame spreading like fire around the school?

"Missed you too."

"I tried some of what we talked about on my mom," he said. "It worked, Logan. I think she actually listened to me for once."

"That's great."

"So maybe it's been my fault all along. When I blurt stuff out, she thinks I'm arguing."

"Do you think I should do her chart?"

He looked impressed. "That's just what I was going to ask you."

We walked in together, and I looked around the room. The usual drama types, probably all Leos, Aries, and Libras, with a sultry Scorpio or almost invisible Cancer in the shadows.

Frankenstein wasn't here yet, no doubt still talking to Snider.

Kat stopped splashing paint on the backdrop against the wall and gave us a confused and angry look. In her paint covered jeans, still holding her brush, she crossed the room toward me.

"Your little game is over," she said. "You're a fake, Astro Girl, and I've figured you out."

"What are you talking about?"

"What don't you understand about fake?" she said. "I know what you're doing. You're so desperate that you convince people their signs are compatible so that you can get guys for your friends." She glared at Nathan, then at me. "*And* for yourself, of course."

"Wait a minute," Nathan said.

The other conversations around the room stopped as if someone had snapped off a radio. I felt myself flush.

"It's all right," I told him. "Kat—"

"I'm not about—," she began. "I refuse to—"

"*I—I—I*," I drowned her out. "*Me—me—me*. You sound just like the double Aries that you are, and an unevolved one at that."

"You're not going to shut me up." Except for her voice, the room remained silent. No one was even pretending to work now. "You were a loser until you reinvented yourself as an astrology expert. Sure, you say you found the Gears, but you have no proof of that. The boys you saw could have been anyone. There's not even any evidence that they were doing anything wrong."

"Because I didn't give them a chance," I said. "They *were* the Gears. I'll stop them the next time they try to strike too." I knew I sounded cocky, but I didn't care.

"It's really gone to your head, hasn't it?" She looked wildly around the room. "Can you see how it's gone to her head? But she's not doing anything, you guys. She's just talking."

"I'm doing, all right," I blurted out. "I happen to know when the Gears are planning their next attack. Now put down that paintbrush, Kat, or I'll put it down for you."

"Bitch." She tossed the dripping thing at me.

I stepped out of the way just in time.

The brush slid across the floor and landed next to Charles Bellamy. I hadn't even realized he was in the room until I watched the bright blue paint splatter all over his shoes.

Nathan yanked the door open. "Mr. Franklin," he shouted. "Where are you?"

"Right here."

Frankenstein stepped inside, all take-charge and scowly. Kat nearly trampled him as she ran out the door.

"Sorry," he said. "Ms. Snider's car is in the shop, and I had to give her a ride home. What's going on here?"

"Kat threw a paintbrush at me," I said. "Look what she did to Charles."

"My shoes." Charles lifted a blue-speckled foot. He sounded stunned.

"Take them off," Frankenstein said. "Maybe we can clean

them. The rest of you kids get back to work. And tomorrow I'm going to have a talk with the vice principal. No one acts like this on my watch."

Everyone but Charles returned to what they'd been doing. I stood beside Nathan, my heart still racing.

"At least she's gone," he said. "Let's hope the rest of the night will be better."

"Knowing Kat," I whispered, "I doubt she'll be gone for long."

"She will." He reached down, squeezed my hand. "You've got to know who Trevor likes, don't you? That's what made Kat crazier than usual."

"I think I know." I smiled up at him. "Confirm it with a first initial, and I'll buy the lattes after we finish painting tonight."

"C." He gave me a one-armed hug. "And *I'll* buy the lattes."

How much better could it get?

"Did you know Trevor was in the parking lot when we pulled in?" I asked.

"Was he? Why?"

He couldn't hide his guilty expression.

"You knew he'd be here, didn't you?"

He shrugged. "He likes C. What can I say?"

"What about Hunter?" I asked.

His expression changed. "Didn't know about him, but Trevor has a right to pick his own friends, I guess."

Another negative about Mr. Aries.

"I guess. In the meantime, what do we do now?"

He picked up the paintbrush that lay where it had landed

before sloshing Charles's shoes. "Work," he said.

"Let's do it," I replied.

We painted late that night. I could feel the other kids looking at me and heard their whispers. I had come on pretty strong about the Gears. Kat had brought out the worst in me. Nathan didn't seem bothered by my outburst, though.

Around ten, Frankenstein finally said, "That's it for tonight, folks. Now get out of here so that I can."

Nathan and I walked out together. My skin tingled in the cold.

Then I saw it.

Right outside the drama classroom, on the opposite wall, was some kind of huge poster. The light shone right down on it. Kids were already gathered around. Their nervous laughter scared me.

Nathan moved closer.

"What is it?" I asked.

"I can't believe it," he said. "They've done it again."

"What do you mean?"

Before he could answer, I saw the words block printed on the huge poster. **SNIDER PUTS OUT 2 HIM.**

At first I just didn't think this was that much worse than previous Gears attacks, but it was.

For those who lacked imagination, intelligence, or both, someone had also pasted blown-up yearbook photos of Snider and Frankenstein on opposite sides of the message.

"Disgusting." I turned to see Charles Bellamy right behind

me. His shoes were clean. "It's really disgusting," he repeated.

Frankenstein shouted from behind him. "Who did this? Get this off the wall, people, and I mean now."

Nathan stood quietly next to me. "Come on," he said, in a calm but firm voice. "I'm going to take you home."

We hurried to the Honda, and I jumped inside.

"Thanks," I said once we were safely out of the parking lot.

"The Gears are such losers." His jaw was set.

I could tell the mood was spoiled.

"Still want coffee?" I tried to smile. "I'm still buying."

"I'll hold you to it next time," he said.

We drove in silence.

He stopped at a red light, and I finally got the courage to ask, "What's wrong, Nathan?"

"The Gears," he said. "They make me sick. This isn't just fun and games anymore. It's cruel."

Something in his voice scared me. He was angrier than I'd ever seen him.

"What is it?" I asked. "You don't know who they are, do you?"

"No," he replied quickly. "Of course not."

But his anger seemed so personal that I couldn't help wondering. No, that was crazy. The Gears were bringing out the paranoia in all of us.

NOTES TO SELF

Nathan was so upset about the Gears that he didn't even kiss me good night. My dad must have sensed that this would be one safe evening. He wasn't out in the driveway dragging around trash cans. Even with all of our newfound privacy in the darkness outside my house, Nathan said only a hasty good-bye. How could I have missed this latest attack? How could I let it happen right after I shot my mouth off? I dread going back to school. I'm going to look like the fake Kat said I was.

28

AS YOU NEAR THE END OF THIS BOOK, CONGRATULATE
YOURSELF ON LEARNING THE BASICS OF ASTROLOGY.
BY NOW, YOU HAVE BEGUN TO TRANSFORM YOUR LIFE.
ASTROLOGY IS NOT EXACT, THOUGH, AND THE MORE
WE LEARN, THE LARGER OUR POTENTIAL FOR ERROR.
THAT'S NO REFLECTION ON YOU. WHEN YOU
ENCOUNTER SETBACKS—AND YOU WILL—DON'T GIVE
UP. JUST GO BACK TO BASICS.

—Fearless Astrology

aybe that's what I needed to do. Go back to basics.
Maybe I'd bounced too rapidly from Sun signs to
Moons, trines, and, worst of all, predictions.

The rumors about Frankenstein and Snider
spread through the school. On both of their classroom doors
the next day, matching posters proclaimed: "Gears Rule."

"I hate this Gears stuff," I told Chili and Paige. "Among other things, I didn't call it, and it's going to back up Kat's claim that I'm a phony."

"No one can be right all the time," Chili said. "You were spot-on about Trevor."

"And Hunter." Paige smiled and hugged herself. "He may be an Aries, but he's a sweet one."

Obviously, their evening had been better than mine. What had gone wrong? Why hadn't the book taught me what to do when understanding astrology wasn't enough to understand life?

"How'd it go with you?" Chili asked.

"Not so great."

"Why?" Paige asked.

"Nathan freaked out about the Gears. I really thought the attack would be Monday, the twenty-fifth. That's when the big disturbance was supposed to occur."

"Maybe something will happen then," Chili said.

"I don't know. I don't trust myself anymore."

Before they could protest—and they were ready to—Kat rushed up and put her face close to mine.

She smelled of mouthwash and strawberry shower gel.

"Hey, Astro Bitch," she said, eyes flashing. "Withdraw my request for a chart, okay?"

"You already have been withdrawn," I told her. "Why are you even in school after what you pulled?"

"I told the vice principal Charles tripped over the

paintbrush." She crossed her hands over her chest, crazy as ever. "I also explained that you were the one making wild claims and disrupting the drama kids."

"That's a lie," I said.

"Of course, but no one will back you up. Everyone's talking about what a loser you are."

"You're the loser, Kat."

Before I could add, *You lost Trevor*, Dina Coulter shoved herself between us.

"Kat's right," Dina said, and tucked a limp strand of black hair behind her ear. "Take me off the list too, Logan. If you knew all you said you do, you would have warned us about what was going to happen after drama. And you would have known the Gears would mess up your column too." Before I could respond, Dina turned to wave at a passing freshman. "Hi, Tiff," she said. "If you want to opt out of the astrology drawing, you can do it here."

Tiff opted out. So did Jared. Chili had been right in the first place. In spite of his looks, he was a drone.

"Sorry," he said. "I know you were my first girlfriend and all, but I've got to do this."

"Not really your first girlfriend," I said. "You were hanging out with Kat that same summer in junior high, weren't you?"

The blush on his face deepened.

"Like I said, sorry." He shrugged. "But no way do I want my name on your list."

"What's the matter?" I said. "Afraid the stars will predict

that your perfect match is an airhead just like you?"

He took off before I could think of anything else.

J.T. was next. "Hey, Logan," he said, towering over me. "Disappear, will you?"

"You'll have to be more specific," I said.

"Take me out of that phony astro drawing, McRae." He smirked and raked his dark hair out of his eyes. "Kat was right about you the whole time."

It continued all day. Most of the kids who'd signed up for a free chart now no longer wanted one. They stopped me in the hall, looked me up in the library and the restroom.

Only Sol, the Texan, who hadn't signed up before, announced to everyone around us, "Put me on that list of yours, Logan."

He, Charles Bellamy, and I shared a large table in journalism. No one else came near. On my way outside after class, Geneva caught up with me.

"Bummer," she said.

Maybe I'd been wrong about her. Our Sun signs were trined, after all. Perhaps our only problem was that we wanted the same boy and the same Monterey fellowship.

Frankenstein asked me to meet with him after the last class. He looked almost cute without his glasses, in his starched little shirt. When had he started wearing white shirts instead of polo pullovers?

"Just wanted you to know that I'm sorry about what's going on," he said. "You're a good kid. The Gears' little poster was outrageous. But it doesn't define me, Logan, not for a moment. Don't let it define you."

"But everyone thinks I'm a phony," I said. "Mr. Franklin, is what happened going to hurt my chances at the fellowship?"

"Of course not. You're a finalist, and that's that. The rest will be based on recommendations, and most of all, the writing."

We talked a little longer, and I started to feel better. True, I wasn't able to predict the next Gears attack. But Frankenstein hadn't turned against me.

I walked out of his classroom toward the parking lot.

Nathan was standing in front of the Honda. When he spotted me, he grinned and opened his arms. I walked over to him.

"You didn't give up on me," I said, and fought the tears I could feel filling my eyes.

"Of course not. You didn't guess the date, but there had to be a reason for it. Maybe I distracted you."

"You didn't," I said. "Somehow I just missed it."

"Don't blame yourself. You'll only make the Gears happier, and they don't deserve that."

We drove around and got something to eat. Later on, when I was calmer, Nathan parked by the river, and we sat there holding hands. Half hidden by the fog, the moon was soft and shimmery, like a slice of yellow melon in the sky.

"I was wrong." I looked up into his eyes. "I never should have convinced myself that I could do this stuff."

"You didn't know." He squeezed my hand, but I wasn't sure about his eyes. Were they so miserable looking because of me or something else? "I still believe in your abilities, Logan."

"You do?"

He nodded. "Trevor's liked Chili since sophomore year. I know you didn't invent fake charts the way Kat said."

"I took all of the information straight from the book," I told him. "Chili and Trevor are compatible. Kat and he are not. For that matter, Kat and anyone probably are not."

"And I still want you to do my mom's chart."

"Well, lucky for you I've got some openings. People aren't exactly standing in line for my services these days."

"I'd stand in line for you any day." His arms went around me. We hugged each other tightly, my head against his sweater, smelling the warmth and the soapy scent I loved. He made me feel that way, that I did have him, that I was protected and somehow safe just as long as he held me like this.

Then we kissed longer and with more passion than we ever had before.

He cared about me, no matter what anyone else thought. And, oh, did I care about him.

"I need to go home," I whispered.

Still holding me, he said, "Can I ask you something really personal, Logan?"

"Of course."

"It's about compatibility."

I pulled away and looked up at him. "What about it?"

"You and me, I mean."

Oh, no. He was asking if he and I were compatible. I could not tell him that I'd been salivating over his chart for weeks.

"Actually, we are." I tried to keep my tone of voice detached, but it was pretty difficult. "In case you didn't notice."

"I noticed, all right." Even in the dark, I could see those turquoise eyes. "Somebody said my best match was supposed to be a Libra."

Geneva. So much for my kind thoughts about her today. She would stoop to anything to get him. At least I hadn't lied to her about the compatibility of Leo and Libra.

"There is no best match," I blurted out, "especially not if there's a lot of Virgo in the Libra's chart."

"Do all Libras have that?"

Caught. His expression was innocent. He didn't know I'd tripped myself up.

"No," I said. "I was just thinking that a Libra with Virgo would be a bad combination for you. Especially with your mom being a Virgo. You have enough of that energy in your life."

"Oh, yeah," he finally said. "How do you know if a Libra has that combination?"

"Just ask. People are almost always proud of what they are." *Especially Geneva.*

"Even when it's bad?"

"Usually, yeah. Even then."

"Don't look so sad," he said. "Everything is going to work out. You still have your friends. You still have *me*."

"Now *you're* the one trying to cheer *me* up," I said. "Nathan, you're the best."

"Why shouldn't I try to cheer you up?" He looked confused.

This wasn't the time to explain about male fire signs and what they needed from their girlfriends.

"I just appreciate it," I said. "That's all I meant."

"I want to be here for you." He kissed me again. "I meant it when I said I believe in you. And I don't think you're going to lose your Star Crossed column either."

"Lose my column?" I repeated. "Where'd you hear that?"

"No one. I mean, nowhere." He shifted in his seat, bit his lip. "I can't remember where I heard it," he finally said. "But I don't believe it."

Leo, I thought, *you are such a terrible liar.*

NOTES TO SELF

Nathan was wrong. I am no longer writing the astrology column for the paper. Snider was kind in the way that those dealing out doom can afford to be. "Nothing to do with you, Logan. We just feel that, considering the circumstances, it's best if we stop the column until the Gears are caught. Geneva is willing to step in for now with a teacher column of her own. It's best for us to play it safe. Don't you agree?" Oh, yes, Snider. I agree all right. Give Geneva my column. Give her anything but my Monterey fellowship. I want that now more than ever.

29

AS YOU'VE LEARNED, THERE'S NO REASON TO FEAR ASTROLOGY. HOWEVER, YOU MUST ALSO BE FEARLESS ABOUT LOVE AND LIFE. BE FEARLESS IN YOUR CHOICES. HEED YOURSELF AS MUCH OR MORE THAN YOU HEED THE INFORMATION PROVIDED HERE. REMEMBER, AS STATED EARLIER, THAT ASTROLOGY IS NOT AN EXACT SCIENCE. STUDY THE STARS, BUT TRUST YOUR HEART.

—Fearless Astrology

I know Nathan heard the news from Geneva. No wonder she looked so sympathetic when she said, "Bummer." I was no longer a threat to her, if I ever was. No, all she felt now was pity. I hated that almost as much as I hated the knowing looks of disgust everyone else was giving me. At least I was invisible before. Now I was visible and pathetic. I so wanted to trust the zodiac, but I didn't know how.

FRANKENSTEIN MUST DIE.

It took a moment for the spray-painted message on that familiar administration office wall to grab my attention. the Gears had gone so far and so crazy that the police made a visit to our campus. Didn't the members of the Gears know that threatening a teacher's life wasn't the same as streaking through a bunch of backyards?

FRANKENSTEIN MUST DIE. I wanted to talk to someone I trusted. I wanted my mom. Although she said I could call anytime, I couldn't, not while she was facing some tough competition on the weekend.

As I headed down the hall that morning, no one seemed to care about the sign. Kat kept grinning like an orthodontic poster child. Dina kept saying, "Hi, Morgan. Hi, Michael. Hi, Sol. Hi, Malik," as if repeating a multicultural telephone book from memory.

"Hi, Chili. Hi, Trevor." Dina stopped for a moment, almost choking as she realized she'd recited the wrong names and far too close together, at that.

"Hi, yourself, lame ass," Chili said.

She and Trevor stood holding hands. They looked as if they belonged together. He wasn't tall, but neither was Chili. His gold-brown curls and her long highlighted hair seemed to blend together in a sunny mass.

As if knowing I was watching her, Chili looked up at me and said, "You're having dinner at my house tonight. My dad will know what to do about that threat."

"He will," Trevor echoed.

Perfect couple. A Gemini and an audience.

Nathan said we needed to talk after school that night, so we met at Java & Jazz. Hunter wasn't there, which again made me wonder what the cute tattooed Aries Paige adored was really doing when he wasn't at work. He and Paige had gone out a couple of times. I shouldn't judge when I didn't know anything about Hunter except that he was a fire sign who missed work now and then.

I reached into my backpack and shoved a folder across the small table.

"Here's your mom's chart, Nathan."

He looked down at it as if it were a filet mignon, and he a carnivore who hadn't eaten in a week.

"I can't," he finally said.

"Why not?"

He couldn't seem to meet my eyes.

"I can't see you anymore." He made it sound like one drawn-out ugly word. Although I knew the meaning in my brain, I needed to feel it in my heart.

"Could you repeat that, Nathan?"

"I can't see you anymore." He pushed the folder back toward me. "Can't take this chart from you either."

I felt tears spring into my eyes, then reached up and wiped them away. "And so because you don't want to go out with me, you don't want the chart I did either?"

"It's not about what I want. I just can't."

So my Nathan fantasy was over. When I looked into his eyes, I saw the same caring there. A pure Leo, too uncomfortable to be telling the truth.

I put my hand over his. "Tell me what's really going on," I said.

"I already told you. It has to be over."

I felt a surge of ridiculous hope. If it was over, that meant there was an *it* to begin with, on his part as well as mine.

"Who says it has to be over? Just tell me what's wrong."

"There's nothing to tell." He pushed back his chair, picked up the full cup, and tossed it into the trash receptacle behind him.

That was a first; the coffee had cost him more than a gallon of gas. I understood, though, because I didn't want mine either. Coffee has a happy smell, and happy didn't make sense right now. I watched Nathan stand and realized that he thought this conversation was over.

"Wait a minute."

He stopped and settled back in his chair. "I told you, Logan—"

"You told me what, but you haven't told me why." Nothing to risk now. I'd already lost him. I picked up my equally full coffee cup and sent it sailing over the table and through the opening of the receptacle. I hoped it crashed into his.

His eyes widened. I could see him trying to hide a smile. "Good shot," he muttered.

"So tell me," I said. "Did you just fall out of whatever you were in with me? Or are you just unable to live with the fact that everyone else in school hates me?"

"It's not that." He looked down as if forgetting that he no longer had a cup beneath him.

"What, then? Please say something so that I don't make a complete fool of myself."

Was I wrong, or did I spot the glimmer of another smile here? "Maybe we can get back together later," he said. "I just need a time-out. I don't want to give you up, though."

I couldn't imagine feeling more humiliated than I did at that moment.

"So when would you like to see me again?" I asked. "Three years from now? Five? Maybe at the twenty-fifth high school reunion?"

"Stop it, will you?" He licked his lips as if making up new lies with every flick of his tongue. "I'll see you in school, of course, but I'll be graduating in less than two months, Logan. Maybe we can get together in June at Chili's folks' place at the lake. Like last year."

June. Two months from now.

"Fun idea," I said sarcastically.

We hadn't been a couple last year. All that had happened were a few late-night swim parties. And, of course, that little matter of Chili stealing Trevor's hoodie.

"That's when I knew I wanted to go out with you," he said. "You were so hot, Logan. I can still see you in that swimsuit."

So much for boys and their memories. I'd been in my shorts and a tank top that week.

"What swimsuit?" I asked.

"The blue one, you know." He flashed me a lazy smile. "You are so hot in those low cut things."

"Nathan." I realized that I was whispering. "I've never worn the suit you just described anywhere but Chili's."

"Wrong," he said. "I've seen you in it."

"Only if you've been to her house. I keep it there. I've never worn it anywhere else."

We stared at each other for a moment. I tried to figure it out. He was breaking up with me. But he'd also just confessed that he'd seen me in a suit that only the naked boys streaking through Chili's backyard could have seen.

"Oh, Nathan," I said. "You're one of the Gears. You are, aren't you?"

"No."

"You are. I know it. The only way you could have seen me in that suit would be in Chili's backyard that night the Gears showed up."

He sat for a moment. "I'm not," he finally said. "Not anymore. I haven't been for a long time."

As I rushed for the door, I realized that Dina and Kat had been watching us from across the room. They laughed loudly as I passed them. I didn't slow down.

Behind me, I heard him shouting, "Logan, wait."

NOTES TO SELF

"Not anymore." What kind of answer is that? Nathan now wants to talk, translation: make excuses for his behavior. I do not. We argued outside the coffee shop loudly enough to give Kat and Dina enough gossip for a week. Finally, my need to learn more about the Gears overrode my feelings of betrayal. It's going to take everything I have to see him tomorrow, though. The one boy, the one person, I'd trusted and believed in was a member of the Gears.

30

ONE OF THE QUICKEST WAYS TO LOSE A LEO IS PUBLIC
HUMILIATION. WITHOUT AN ADORING AUDIENCE, LEO
IS SELDOM HAPPY AND PROBABLY NOT AROUND FOR
LONG. IF YOU WANT TO KEEP THAT LION IN THE LAIR,
AVOID PUBLIC DISPLAYS OF ANYTHING BUT ADORATION.

—Fearless Astrology

ell, my Leo had his share of public humiliation last night, and Kat and Dina had gotten more
show than they bargained for. The last thing I
wanted was coffee with him, but if I could find out anything
about the Gears, it would be worth it.

I had reluctantly agreed to meet him at his house. He
probably didn't want to be seen in public with me, and after
the drama last night, I wasn't all that excited about going
anywhere with him either.

Nathan's brother opened the door and smiled up at me
from his wheelchair. Except for the shiny blond curls, he

could have been Nathan's twin. Another Leo. I'd bet my astrology book on it.

"I'm Logan," I said, and stepped inside.

"Jeremy," he replied. "Nathan's in charge of the breakfast burritos, and I'm toasting the bagels. But don't worry, I've got to study, so you two can have some privacy."

What was he talking about?

"I just came by for coffee."

"Whatever," he said, and moved toward what had to be the kitchen.

This house wasn't what I'd expected. I'd always pictured something cozy and warm with a fireplace and hardwood floors. A safe retreat for Nathan and his brother. Instead, what waited for me was an interior designer's stark dream of what a home should look like. White leather sofas, black cushions, and vibrant art were surrounded by large windows overlooking the koi pond.

I followed Jeremy into the kitchen. Nathan looked up from the granite-covered countertop.

"Breakfast burritos." He grinned. "You'll love them."

"I came to talk," I said. "That's all."

"Okay, okay. I just thought . . ."

"Algebra calls," Jeremy said, and grabbed a bagel from the toaster. "I'm going to my room. Have fun, guys."

"You don't want to eat?" Nathan asked once his brother had disappeared down the hall.

"No." I leaned against the kitchen counter and pushed the

butter dish out of my way. "I want to hear your explanation for all this."

He looked down at the burritos in the pan as if he were the one who'd been betrayed.

"So, I was a Gear. It started out as a joke, just for fun, like acting in a play. I got out of it as soon as you and I started seeing each other."

I guess he expected me to consider that an honorable act.

"Was it hard to leave the group?" I asked. "Did the others threaten you?"

"You wouldn't believe how hard." He sighed. "Let's just say they weren't very happy. I tried to get them to stop too. They wouldn't, though—still won't."

I could tell he was liking his own story now, writing it like a screenplay where he was the hero.

I walked around the counter and leaned across it. "Who are the other Gears, Nathan?"

He shook his head, unconvinced by what I hoped was my conspiring tone. "It wouldn't help, you know. It might actually hurt you."

"Hunter," I said. "He's one of them, isn't he?"

"No way." He looked almost as miserable as Charles Bellamy had when Frankenstein accused him of being responsible for what happened to my column. "Hunter is a musician. He's different. Weird in a way, but he knows who he is."

"And he's not a Gear?"

"Wouldn't have the time if he wanted to be. He works like

five jobs and goes to school part-time."

Maybe that was the reason Hunter was out sick from work at the coffee shop. Wrong again, Logan.

"The Gears can't hurt me any more than they already have," I said. "Why can't you tell me who they are? Are you afraid of them?"

"Why would I want to rat out my friends?" He looked away, and I could tell I'd gotten to him.

"Because," I said. "You can help undo a lot of damage. It's way past streaking now. You guys said that Frankenstein must die."

"We didn't do that. We don't know who left that message, Logan, but it wasn't us. We'd never threaten a teacher's life."

Of course not. Just mature stuff like stealing mailboxes, streaking, and spray-painting the administration office with *SNIDER PUTS OUT*. That's all.

"There can't be two Gears groups." I reached down and lifted my backpack into my lap.

"That's what *we* said." This time, he didn't attempt to hide his smile. "Guess that's what's going on, though. You aren't the only one to suspect Hunter."

"So you do think he's involved?" Poor Paige.

"I don't," Nathan said. "Like I said, he's different, but I don't think he's one of them."

"Then who in the Gears suspects him?" I asked, but he closed himself off again.

I looked at his perfect face, those lips I'd been so psyched to kiss. It was all I could do to keep from crying.

"Will you at least tell me how you guys worked?" I asked. "Did you pick your dates in advance, or did you just do whatever felt right?"

"There was a schedule," he said. "What would happen, and when. I can tell you that much."

"How far ahead did you know about it?"

"Sometimes days, sometimes hours." He reached out across the counter for my hand, but I drew back. "What are you doing?" he asked.

"Checking something out." I took the book out and opened it. Although Leos weren't known for lying, this one might be. I needed to do some research, and I didn't care that he was watching.

"Would you listen to me?" he said. "I invited you over today because I want to make it right. I want to make *us* right. I'm not going to give you details, though, and I'm not going to give you names. If you decided to talk, some of us wouldn't be able to graduate."

Which meant that some of them were seniors. And he was afraid of them. Combined with the fact that he didn't seem to want to break up with me and didn't want anyone to know that he was seeing me this morning. A sickening little feeling spread through me. I skipped to the familiar Libra page covered with my sticky notes.

"That's for sure." I grabbed his arm. "Whoever sabotaged my article was one of the Gears, right?"

"Yeah," he said. "I can't tell you who that was, though."

"You don't have to." I stood up and looked into those eyes I adored. "You've told me enough."

He grabbed my hand. I pulled away, and his own hand slammed into the butter. The dish shattered on the floor. I stood there for a moment, torn between staying here and trying to make it better, or leaving and doing what I had to do. If I stayed, he might try to convince me that I was wrong, that what I suspected was just my certifiable overactive imagination. If I stayed, I might let him.

NOTES TO SELF

With *Fearless Astrology*, I should be able to figure out the rest of what I need to know. Why someone would do this. How to get them to confess. I have to figure it out too. Everything I believe in depends on it. Only one person could have both sabotaged my article and orchestrated the naked run through Chili's backyard. Only one person in this school is smart enough to organize a bunch of guys and get away with it. And only one person has a motive for pushing Nathan into breaking up with me. My next job will be to find out where she is today and make her admit it.

31

EVERY SIGN TELLS A LIE NOW AND AGAIN, BUT SOME ARE MORE LIKELY TO THAN OTHERS. THE OUTSPOKEN LEOS USUALLY PREFER TO SAY WHAT'S ON THEIR MINDS RATHER THAN RESORT TO FALSEHOODS. THAT DOESN'T MEAN THEY'RE AS BLATANT AS ARIES OR AS HOOF-IN-MOUTH AS BLURTING SADGE. ALL FIRE SIGNS THINK THEY KNOW BEST. THEIR PHILOSOPHY TENDS TO BE: WHY LIE? GEMINI, PISCES, SCORPIO, AND LIBRA MAY TEND TO STRETCH THE TRUTH A BIT MORE THAN SOME OTHER SIGNS, BUT FOR DIFFERENT REASONS. PISCEANS ARE FUNNY ABOUT PRIVACY. THEY WILL LIE JUST TO KEEP OTHERS FROM KNOWING WHAT THEY ARE THINKING OR DOING. GEMINIS TEND TOWARD WHITE LIES AIMED AT HELPING OR NOT GETTING IN TROUBLE. THEY USUALLY END UP GETTING IN ONLY

DEEPER. SCORPIOS LIE TO AVOID SPILLING THEIR
SECRETS. LIBRAS LIE BY OMISSION—WHICH CAN OFTEN
GET OTHERS INTO TROUBLE.

—*Fearless Astrology*

That's what she'd done this whole time, lied by omission, by what she hadn't said. It was time for a confrontation. I knew she ran laps on Saturday. Everyone in school did, and any number of boys would show up to run with her. Today, she was alone.

"Hey, Geneva," I shouted across the football field.

She stopped, squinted at me, and called back, "What?"

I motioned to where I stood and said, "Can you come over here?"

She jogged in my direction. The sweat trickling through her pale hair and running down her forehead made her look younger and somehow less secure.

"So what's so urgent?" she asked. "If it's about the column, I didn't ask to replace it with my own. Considering the way the Gears have been acting, Snider and I just figured this might be best for a while."

"It's not about the column."

"What, then?" she asked, still running in place.

"The Gears," I replied.

Her expression didn't change. "What about them?"

"You were all too happy to give me an alibi when they trashed my column, weren't you?"

"Why wouldn't I be? I did see you that Friday night in the parking lot getting into that *vehicle* of yours."

"But I didn't see you getting into yours." This time I got a reaction out of her. She stopped jogging and glared at me. "You were setting up an alibi when you said we had left the journalism room together."

"No doubt another lame theory based on something you read in that book."

"In a way, yes," I said. "After checking out where your Mars and Venus are, I can see why you might enjoy the power of bossing around a bunch of boys and terrorizing the school."

"Oh, I get it." She stepped back and gave me that snide Geneva look. "So now that Nathan's dumped you, you're so desperate that you're willing to accuse anyone."

"Not anyone." I kept my voice calm, no longer afraid of her. "What makes you think Nathan dumped me?"

"Gossip." She looked me up and down as if that scrutiny should make me uncomfortable. "I was sorry to hear about the breakup. You're both nice people."

"Yes we are," I said. "And since you're so sorry about the breakup, I'm sure you'll be thrilled to know that he still wants us to be together."

"He does?" The cat eyes blinked, then studied me with

renewed interest. "Um, have you seen him recently?"

"This morning at his house," I said. "And, yes, we are very much together. He told me who the leader of the Gears is."

She straightened as if to make herself even taller. "I'm so glad you worked it out, especially with all you've been dealing with lately. I don't think Snider will want to give you the column back, though."

"Do you think she'll be interested in learning who's the brains behind the Gears?"

"If you can prove it." A slow smile spread over her face. "And you can't prove it, can you?"

"Maybe," I said. "I'd sure like to know why you did it, though."

I watched her skin change. Not a downright sweat, but a definite sheen. She was more worried than she was pretending to be.

"Why I did what?" she asked, and I could tell she was fighting to keep her tone friendly.

"Why would someone like you, someone beautiful, smart, and talented, want to do what you've done?"

She glowed at the compliment. Typical Libra. Then she said, "Why wouldn't I? Not that I'm admitting anything, understand."

"But suppose I'm right, and you are what I think you are? Tell me this. If you did it, what would be your reason?"

Her grin was slow and steady. "Logan, do you have any idea how boring my life is? How boring my parents are? Not to mention my little brother and his stupid friends."

"A lot of kids have less than boring, you know." Before I finished speaking, I realized that she had given me the rest of the puzzle pieces. Jared was the little brother. And the friends she mentioned? Jared had only one, that string bean J.T.

"So you decided to stir things up, didn't you, big sister? Get Jared and J.T. doing your dirty work."

"Maybe."

"How'd Nathan get involved?"

"If you were really as close as you pretend, he would have told you."

"There's no pretending. I know his reasons."

I did, too. Nathan needed to be on stage. The Gears gave him much of the attention he wasn't getting at home.

All of the pieces began clicking into place. All but one.

"I know boys can be idiots," I said, "but Nathan isn't mean. Neither are Jared and J.T."

"What do they have to do with it?"

I could have told her that she just gave me the clues. Instead, I said, "Astrology. I know what you've done. What I can't figure out is why you would encourage something like *Frankenstein Must Die*."

"I didn't have anything to do with that."

"But you did. You made the Gears write it. How could you be so evil?"

"Logan," she said. "Whatever else you believe about the situation, please believe me on this one. The Gears are not responsible for *Frankenstein Must Die*. They don't know anything."

"Do you—I mean, they—do they have any idea who's after Frankenstein?"

"Maybe," she said. "You know how tough he can be. There's a former student of his attending JC now who absolutely hates him. I know because I talk to the guy at the coffee shop."

"Hunter Allen?" I asked.

"All I'll tell you is that Hunter isn't a member of the Gears. If he's leaving threats all over the place, he'd better make it clear that he's acting independently."

Hunter. There he was again. I had to find out if he was the one threatening Frankenstein's life. For Paige's sake, I hoped he'd turn out to be innocent. He was an Aries. But how much of an Aries?

"Um, can we consider this conversation over?" Geneva stared out at the field, then back to me.

"Sure," I said. "If I tell anyone what we've discussed out here, you're going to say I'm lying, right?"

"Absolutely." She moved closer to me. "If you even think about talking about what you think I did, I'll just explain how you started this whole phony astrology thing, and how the kids can't stand you. You won't a chance."

"And you'd do that?" My voice felt raw.

"If I have to. I'm out of here, Logan. Your best bet is to just leave me alone. Leave the Gears alone too. We'd all like to catch whoever left the threat, but so far, that's not happening."

"Can I ask you one more thing?"

She shrugged. "If you ask it fast."

How could I ever have thought she was cool?

"Snider," I said. "She took an interest in you. Tried to give you every break, credited you with the newspaper's success. How could you have let your brother and his friend post that awful stuff about her?"

"All's fair," she said. In that moment I realized that I was not just staring into the face of cool. I was staring into cold.

NOTES TO SELF

Whatever is wrong with Geneva goes beyond astrology. She feels no remorse. No guilt. That calm look in her eyes scared me more than the manic craziness in Kat's. So now I know who the Gears are: Geneva, her brother, Jared, his friend J.T., and until recently, Nathan. If Nathan is to be believed, of course, and Leos usually can be. According to what I learned from the ephemeris, something bad could happen on Monday. Could that be related to **FRANKENSTEIN MUST DIE**? Nathan and Geneva both claim they don't know who's behind it. What am I going to do?

32

THERE IS A TIME WHEN EVERYONE MUST DEPEND ON
SOMEONE ELSE. AT SUCH TIMES, IT IS IMPORTANT TO
TRUST ONE'S FRIENDS. THAT IS, IF YOU KNOW WHICH
ONES ARE THE FRIENDS, WHICH ONES ARE THE IN
DIFFERENTS, AND WHICH ARE THE ENEMIES IN
DISGUISE. SELECT CAREFULLY AND ACT ACCORDINGLY.

—*Fearless Astrology*

didn't speak until Chili, Paige, and I were on the
Chiliderians' deck, sitting around the patio
table. Stella had brought out a platter of *yalanchi*,
her stuffed marinated grape leaves, and a bunch of paper
towels folded on a separate plate.

"Use the towels after you eat the *yalanchi*, girls," she said.
"Olive oil messes up the pool filter."

Before leaving, she knelt beside me.

"You doing okay, honey?"

"Fine," I said, and tried to look that way.

"Years from now . . ." she tapped my shoulder with her shiny acrylics, ". . . this column of yours . . . this silly boy . . . they are going to seem so unimportant."

She was trying to make me feel better and had no idea how to. Still, I loved her for trying.

I squeezed her hand with my oily fingers. "Thanks, Stella."

"Don't do anything crazy, Logan. Promise me that."

"I won't," I said.

Not until Monday, that is.

Once she made her way back into the house, we all sat there looking at one another. Then we got up and found our places around the spa. Chili and Paige, both in cover-ups, moved closer to me, one on each side, as if trying to protect me from a disease I'd already caught.

"Finally," Chili said once Stella had closed the door. "What's going on, Logan?"

"I know who the Gears are."

"You do?" She and Paige both shrieked.

"Unfortunately, yes."

Chili bounced up and down. "What do you mean, *unfortunately*? How can it be a bad thing that you've found the Gears? Oh, this is so exciting."

"It is and it isn't." I slid down and let my legs stretch and relax in the warmth of the spa. When I looked up, I saw fear on Paige's delicate, pale face. "Don't be afraid," I said.

"Just tell me Hunter's not one of them," she blurted.

I couldn't reveal my suspicions now. It wouldn't be fair. "I can only say that Hunter's not one of the boys who streaked through here that night." I pointed in the direction the Gears had come.

"Thank goodness." Paige sighed, and I was glad I hadn't said more. "Well, who did, then?"

Chili grabbed my arm. "Not Trevor?"

"No," I said. "Jared Hamilton."

Both of them gasped.

"Ew," Chili said. "To think Geneva's creepy brother saw me almost naked."

"Jared was more naked. The other is J.T."

A new round of screams erupted.

"Who else?" Paige asked. "There were three."

How could I handle this one? *Just say it*, I told myself.

"Nathan." My lip began to tremble. They both grabbed me at once.

"Oh, Logan," Chili said.

Paige hugged me with one arm. "I was so afraid you were going to say Hunter. I can't imagine how you must feel. Nathan seems so nice."

"He is nice, and he's not a Gear anymore," I said. "But he was one of the three here that night. He told me. And listen to this. Geneva is the leader."

"Geneva?" they shouted in unison.

"She admitted it," I said.

"Oh, Logan," Chili said, "you're going to be all right now.

Just think. You're bringing down the Gears and exposing Geneva for what she really is."

"I don't know." I stared down at my legs, like pale streaks in the water.

"What do you mean you don't know?" Chili said. "You have to tell."

"But if she tells . . ." Paige's voice was soft. "Nathan is caught right along with the rest of them."

"So don't mention his name," Chili said. "If the Gears turn him over, that's not your problem. Besides, you said he's out now."

"I don't know if that's the right thing to do," I said. "Besides, Geneva already said she'll deny it."

"Let her." Chili splashed the water with her foot. "You're telling the truth, Logan. Someone will listen to you. Snider will, I know it."

"You have to try," Paige said. "Otherwise, something awful could happen."

"She's right," Chili said.

I glanced from one to the other. They both looked excited, as if convinced that I could do this.

"I guess I don't have any choice, do I?"

They shook their heads.

"You've got to," Chili said, "and before Monday night."

NOTES TO SELF

Chili and Paige are right. I'm going to have to tell Snider what's going on. She cares about Frankenstein, I'm sure of it. If she knows he's going to be in danger Monday night, maybe she can help me figure out who is behind **FRANKENSTEIN MUST DIE.** It will probably cost me whatever's left of my relationship with Nathan, but he lied to me. I can't think about him right now. I've got to stop whoever is after Frankenstein.

33

The Water Bearer, which is the sign of Aquarius, shows a man pouring water from a jug, which is a symbol of the divine spirit watering the earth. Although later depicted as a woman, the figure is male, and, along with the other Fire and Air signs, Aquarius is Masculine. Those born under Masculine signs are more prone to bluntness. They also lean toward being detached and un involved but are, at heart, true humanitarians. When most Aquarians are caught in difficult situations, they will usually put self aside and do what they believe is right.

—*Fearless Astrology*

hat's where I was right now, trying to do the right thing. Although I got to Snider's room early that morning, a bunch of kids were already huddled around her desk. When I told her I needed to talk to her and would be back that afternoon, I got only a stony look in response. I still had to try. It was the twenty-fifth, and she was my only hope to stop whatever might happen to Frankenstein.

It's amazing how when one influential kid decides you're not cool, everyone else in school gets the message. Talk about viral. This must be what Charles Bellamy had to live with every day. He and Sol sat by me in journalism as the other kids moved as far away as possible. Through the window, I could see Paige waiting outside, but I needed to talk to Charles first.

"Got a minute?" I asked. He gave me an uncertain nod, and I said, "Thank you for not turning against me."

His face flushed deeper. "I have to go to auto shop now."

"I know who you were with that night the Gears destroyed my column."

He stopped as if I'd punched him.

"She said she liked me. I wouldn't have believed it, only she knew about my dad, and we talked about him a lot." I could see him try to swallow. "She said I was interesting. I'm sorry about your column, Logan."

"While you two were in the back room, her brother and J.T. came in and destroyed my layout," I said. "I'm going to Ms. Snider after school. Charles, please help me."

"I can't." He chewed on his lower lip. "You don't understand." His face grew even redder. "I can't," he repeated, then bolted from the room before I could try to convince him.

I met up with Paige, and we began walking to our next class.

"What's up with Charles?" she asked.

"He's really upset," I told her. "Geneva used him to give her brother and J.T. a chance to mess up my column that Friday we went to San Francisco. He refuses to tell anyone, though."

"He looked in bad shape."

"I guess he's embarrassed that he believed Geneva liked him. He's still willing to lie for her. I've got to change his mind about that."

"He had tears in his eyes when he ran past me," Paige said. "I'd be surprised if he makes it through the rest of the day."

"He's got to. I need him to come with me when I talk to Snider."

Paige was right. No one saw Charles after journalism, and Chili said he checked into auto shop later but left before class was over.

Paige and Chili must have agreed to take turns waiting for me after my classes. One of them was always at my side, as if to dare the rest of the kids to confront me. I loved them more than ever.

"Want us to meet you in Snider's room?" Chili asked.

"Better not," I said. "It would look as if I can't speak for myself."

"All right, then, if you're sure. We'll wait for you in the

parking lot."

After my last class, I returned to Snider's room. She was cool and more reserved than usual. Her white shirt looked as if she'd just ironed it.

"Have a seat, Logan," she said without moving from her desk.

I pulled up a chair and forced myself to sit. "Ms. Snider, I know who the Gears are."

She nodded, no surprise showing in her expression. "Do you?"

"Yes," I said. "Jared Hamilton and J.T. Malone. Geneva's in charge." I just couldn't do it to Nathan. Let the Gears take care of that.

"Geneva's already come to see me." She studied my face as if watching for my reaction. "I understand you two had a conversation about Geneva substituting her column for yours, and about Nathan Sullivan as well."

"We had a conversation, all right," I said. "I asked Geneva how she could allow her brother and J.T. to post such awful stuff after you were so kind to her. Do you know what she said? '*All's fair.*' That's really what she believes about what she's done."

She straightened up in her prim little shirt. "What you're saying is very difficult to believe, especially since Geneva told me that you threatened to do something like this."

"There's one person who can back me up," I said. "Charles Bellamy. He was with her in the copy room the night my column was trashed."

She grimaced. "Charles and Geneva?"

"I know that sounds unlikely," I said, "but it was the only way the Gears could ruin my column."

"Logan." She stood. "This has to stop. If you're going to make such outrageous accusations, you need proof. Charles confides in me, and he's never mentioned anything like that. If he really experienced what you're suggesting, I want to hear it from him. Both of you be here before class tomorrow."

"Tomorrow's too late." I got up and tried to ignore her distrustful expression. "Something's going to happen to Mr. Franklin tonight. We have to stop it now."

"That's ridiculous," she said. "Nothing is going to happen to Mr. Franklin."

"But the ephemeris . . . How can you be so sure I'm wrong? The poster was real enough, and whoever put that up is going to cause more trouble tonight."

"Is she?" Ms. Snider asked. "Geneva and I discussed that too. I can assure you Mr. Franklin is safe. Now, I want you to go home. If you insist on continuing this talk tomorrow, you and Charles can meet with me then."

She? Was Snider suggesting that I was responsible for the poster? The Capricorn had made up her mind. Geneva had lied just as she'd said she would, and now Snider actually believed my accusations were based on jealousy.

"Fine," I said, and left the room without another word.

Chili and Paige were waiting as they'd promised. I climbed in beside Chili.

"Well?" she asked.

"Snider didn't believe me," I said, and burst into tears.

"It's okay." Chili hugged me, and Paige rubbed my shoulders. "Geneva's bragging that you're spreading lies about her because you're jealous that she's writing a column and you aren't."

"What am I going to do? If Snider won't listen to me, I have to find someone who will."

"My mom?" Chili asked.

"But what would she do? She'd just call my dad, and they'd make me stay home tonight."

"You aren't going to try to stop them by yourself again, are you?"

"I've got to." I wiped my eyes. "There's no other way."

Chili reached over and blotted my lashes with a tissue. "Then I'm going with you."

"You can't."

"Me too," Paige said. "And, yes, we can. We're going to do this together, Logan, or not at all."

NOTES TO SELF

I did the right thing just the way most Aquarians would in times of trouble, and instead my situation is worse than before. Snider thinks I'm a liar. Frankenstein probably agrees. I have as big a chance of getting the fellowship as Charles has of taking Geneva to the prom. But I have two friends who aren't going to let me do what I have to do alone. Whoever is behind **FRANKENSTEIN MUST DIE** is going to have to deal with the three of us tonight.

34

NEVER UNDERESTIMATE THE POWER OF VENUS. NEXT
TO THE SUN AND MOON, SHE IS THE BRIGHTEST OBJECT
IN OUR SKY. YOU WILL FEEL HER POWER WHEN YOU
EXPERIENCE DEEP AND OFTEN SUDDEN ATTRACTION TO
ANOTHER PERSON. YOU ALSO FEEL IT WHEN YOUR LOVE
FOR ANOTHER GROWS, SOMETIMES OUT OF CONTROL.
THOSE WITH VENUS IN CANCER MAY WANT LOVE BUT
FIND IT DIFFICULT TO OBTAIN. YET IT IS IMPOSSIBLE TO
RESIST THE GODDESS.

—Fearless Astrology

We came up with a plan on the way home. We
would take my dad's paint van, because it was less
obvious than Chili's car. In the meantime, I worked
on the chart for Charles. If I could figure out a little more about
him, maybe I could get him to tell the truth to Ms. Snider.

"His Venus is in Cancer," I said. "That sure fits. He's probably built Geneva into a goddess of love, and he's not about to rat her out."

We were in Paige's bedroom with Calypso. Paige was arranging a low-slung belt around the mannequin's hips. "Where are we going to start looking?" she said. "Who are our suspects?"

"Geneva, of course, in spite of what she says about it being someone outside the Gears." Chili got up and rearranged the belt. "You're making Calypso look too top-heavy, Paige."

"Geneva isn't about to risk getting caught," I told her. "If the Gears are involved, she'll make her brother and J.T. do it. Whatever it is."

"What about Nathan?" Paige asked in a soft voice.

"He says he's finished. He's too scared to see me again, let alone come forward about the Gears. Besides, I really think he believes the *Frankenstein Must Die* thing isn't the work of the Gears."

"Who, then?" Chili asked.

Paige stopped fussing with Calypso. "Hunter doesn't like Frankenstein," she said slowly. "He said they fought all through his senior year."

I sat on the bunk bed. "Geneva told me they think it's Hunter."

"No," Paige said in disbelief. "Hunter did say that Frankenstein deserved all the harassment he was getting. Do you think he could be behind this?"

"I don't know," I said. "He's an Aries, fire sign, but so are lots of decent people. Do you know where he is tonight?"

"He's supposed to be working at Java & Jazz."

"Want to find out?"

Before she could answer, Chili was out the door, heading for the garage.

I took Paige's arm. "Are you all right with this? Because if you aren't, you can stay here."

"I'm with you guys," she said. "I want to know too."

Java & Jazz was in the mall. We pulled into the parking lot behind it. "That's Hunter's truck," Paige whispered from the back. "Thank goodness. I was so afraid it was him."

So my astrology skills had failed me one more time. "We're going to have to think of something else."

"Maybe we can just go to wherever Frankenstein is and hang out," Chili said.

"But how do we know where Frankenstein is?"

She giggled. "Where do you think?"

"Snider?" She had sounded pretty smug today when I told her he was in danger. "We could just drive by her place and see if his car's there."

"It won't be," Chili said. "He left it in auto shop for detailing right after school today. You know how obsessed he is with it. He could buy a new car for what he spends on Armor All alone."

"It's his baby, that's for sure." The moment the words were out, my flesh tingled. *It's his baby.* "Who all was around when he brought it in?" I asked, my voice trembling and my mind racing ahead. "Who knows it's there?"

"Just Charles and me. He's the only one good enough to detail for Frankenstein." She glanced over at me. "What is it?"

"The school," I said. "Hurry."

She swung out of the parking lot, and we were off. By the dim light of the glove box, I paged through the book, trying to prove myself wrong about Charles. "Mars in Scorpio," I said. "A risk taker. Oh, no. What if Geneva's telling the truth for once, and the Gears didn't leave that poster? What if it was Charles?"

"Why would he do that?" Paige shouted. It was the only way to be heard in the van.

"Venus. I mean, love. Oh, my god, it's not Geneva he's crushing on. It's Snider. Have you ever seen how he looks at her? Now, thanks to the Gears, everyone knows she's with Frankenstein. Charles was there the night that we were painting sets too."

"But Charles is a wimp," Paige said. "He wouldn't kill Frankenstein."

"No." Chili screeched to a stop at a red light and turned to me. "But he'd kill his car, wouldn't he?"

She took off again, and I was slammed back against my seat.

"What if Charles has flipped out? We've got to call a teacher, anyone who can help us."

"There's no one who will believe us," Chili said.

"No one," Paige echoed. "Geneva has tried to turn practically everyone against you."

Just then I closed my eyes and saw frizzy red curls, penetrating eyes.

"Jillian Berry," I shouted.

"You're crazy," Chili said. "What makes you think that weirdo would believe you?"

"Because she *is* a weirdo. Because she doesn't care what people think about her. And because she likes me."

Berry did like me, I knew. I still had her card in my book bag. On our way to the school, I phoned her. She answered on the first ring.

"Ms. Berry, this is Logan McRae," I said. "I know this is going to sound crazy, but please listen to me. I found the Gears, but no one will believe me. And now, I'm pretty sure that Charles Bellamy is at the high school auto shop. I think he's going to destroy Mr. Franklin's Corvette."

She paused for a moment, then said, "I believe you, Logan. Now listen to me, honey. I'll handle it from here. Don't go near the shop."

Just then the line went dead, which was just as well.

"What'd she say?" Chili asked.

"She believes me." My voice broke. "Now hurry. We can't let this happen."

I wasn't sure just then what I was trying to prevent. Charles ruining Frankenstein's car or Charles ruining Charles. I only knew that we couldn't stop now.

The overhead lights were off, but I could see a glow inside.

We pulled around in back. Charles's car was the only one in the lot.

Paige gasped. My skin crawled.

"Let me out here," I said.

Chili shook her head. "We're coming with you."

"If I go alone, I might have a chance," I told her. "It's the only way."

Before she could reply, I opened the door and jumped out.

The inside light was dim and watery, not modern like the other classrooms or labs. That's because most of the overheads were off. The first thing I saw when I stepped inside was a stack of four fancy tires. Beside them was Frankenstein's Corvette, minus the wheels. Charles walked from the back shop. He was wearing a white lab coat and surgical-type mask. Whatever he had in the can he was holding smelled foul.

"Charles, wait."

"Get out of here, Logan. I mean it."

"Take off your mask and talk to me." I coughed. "What's in that thing?"

"Chemicals you shouldn't be breathing. You need to leave."

"You're going to get caught," I said.

"I don't care." His eyes looked dead. He glared down at the Corvette with its perfect yellow paint, its creamy leather upholstery. "I hate him."

"No you don't. You hate that he has something you want."

"You don't understand."

"I do. I know what it's like to care about someone. You

aren't the only one who wants someone he can't have."

He paused and seemed to consider the can again.

"At least I could pretend I had her, that I would have her someday." He moved close to the car, lifted the can.

"You can still pretend. That's what I do." Tears squeezed out onto my cheeks. I kept talking. "My mom will come home for good after the next tour. That's what I tell myself. Even though it's not real, it makes me feel better."

"You pretend?" He took a step back, and I moved closer. "About your mom?"

"Every day. You know how it feels to have a famous parent. You know how lonely it can be to have to act like it doesn't matter that they're somewhere else more than they're with you." I moved closer as I spoke. "It's okay to pretend when your life feels shitty and messed up."

"It's so shitty," he said. "So messed up."

"Mine too." I got a firm grip on the can. "Now give me that and take off the mask. Then we'll figure out what to do."

His fingers slowly released the can. I placed it on the ground, and he took off his mask, carefully, as if he were sleepwalking. Under the light his tears made silver streaks down his face. I put out my arms, and he let me hug him, sobbing like a child. I cried too. For his losses, for mine, and because I didn't know how to fix life for either one of us.

"It's going to be all right," I said over and over. He was still holding on to me when they came for him.

NOTES TO SELF

Jillian Berry had gone into action the minute our call was disconnected. Dr. West arrived about the same time she did. The school psychologist showed up shortly thereafter. Other people too. Chili and Paige, and all of a sudden, my dad and Stella. I knew I was out of control, sobbing as hopelessly as Charles. But even then, clinging to my dad, I knew that I was safe. All I can remember saying is, "Don't let them hurt him."

35

THE TIME HAS COME FOR YOU TO EVALUATE WHAT YOU'VE LEARNED THUS FAR. LIST THE MOST IMPORTANT DISCOVERY YOU'VE MADE WHILE WORKING THROUGH THIS BOOK.

—*Fearless Astrology*

Knowing someone's sign does not mean I know the person. It's only a starting place.

Good friends can get you through just about anything.

Most guys like to feel important. So do most girls, for that matter, regardless of their signs.

Things don't always work out according to my plan, but they work out.

The Sun is not the sum.

Yes, I know that's more than one discovery, but it's the best I can do for now.

—Logan McRae

Once more I made the transition from scumbag to star. Thanks to Jillian Berry and my friends, everyone knew that I had saved Frankenstein's Corvette from an acid bath. When I walked down the hall that day, kids grinned. A couple congratulated me.

Dina walked toward me with an expectant look on her face. Once I'd passed her, I heard a hasty "Hiii, Logan." I was back on top, but this part of fake cool I could do without.

Snider got up from her desk and walked over to me when I came into the room. "I'm sorry," she said. "I was so wrong to doubt you."

"You believe me now?" I asked. "About the Gears?"

She nodded. "Charles told us what happened. Nathan backed him up and added more details."

I couldn't help grinning. Nathan had come forward.

"What's going to happen to the Gears and Charles?" I asked.

She shook her head. "We'll have to see. It's up to Dr. West."

Nathan wasn't at school. Neither were Geneva, Jared, or J.T.

Poor Nathan. All he wanted was a little attention and maybe Geneva's approval. And now he was in trouble. I hoped he'd be able to graduate. Yes, I still cared about him.

Frankenstein was at his desk when I walked in. He wore a light blue shirt that contrasted with his tan, and his eyes were clear.

"I was hoping you'd come early," he said. "I want to thank you for saving my car. I know that sounds silly."

"No, it doesn't. I feel awful about Charles, though."

"He's going be all right," he said. "His mother is here, and from what I understand, she'll be taking him home with her to Southern California. You did the right thing to stop him."

"I hope so."

"You know what this means, don't you?" he asked. "He and Geneva are both disqualified for the fellowship. You're our only remaining finalist."

I hadn't even thought about that. Now I could hardly control myself. "I can't believe it. What do I have to do?"

"Plenty." His gruff voice turned him into Frankenstein again. "Don't think I'm going to hand this to you, McRae. You still need a killer writing sample, and none of your essays are there yet. Do you have anything else? Something written from the heart?"

Then I remembered what I did have. I couldn't possibly, though. There was too much in it. Besides, he'd know I called him *Frankenstein*.

"What?" he demanded.

"No, it's too crazy."

"Why? You do have something, don't you?"

"I do, but, well, it's really personal."

"McRae," he said. "What have I been trying to tell you since the first day of class? Personal is good."

"But—"

"Good," he repeated, and held out his hand. "And if for some reason it's not, I'll be the only one who ever sees it. You can trust me to keep my mouth shut. I won't even share it with Brooke."

As in Ms. Snider. I was speechless. What had he just openly admitted to me?

"It's handwritten," I finally said.

"I think you know how to use a computer." He stood, his attitude pure challenge.

"I sure do," I said.

He was back in charge. This time I was going to give him what he wanted.

NOTES TO SELF

Dear Mr. Franklin: You said you wanted personal. Well, I've never written anything as personal as this journal. Sorry for the nickname, but you know that's what most of us call you. I'm not sure when I stopped thinking of it as a bad name. Maybe that day you gave me a second chance at my personal essay. I know you're on my side, Mr. Franklin, and I'm not trying to use astral manipulation on you either. At least I don't think I am. Sincerely, Logan

36

Congratulations. You have completed the first volume in this series and are now ready for *Fearless Astrology, Volume II*. May this initial investigation of the planets and the Zodiac enrich and deepen your life. More self-discovery and enlightenment lie ahead. Onward and inward.

—*Fearless Astrology*

"What are you doing with those boxes, honey?"

"Looking for something, Dad."

In the office, with the contents of the closet spread to every corner of the room, I hear him come inside. Seeing him relaxed and in jeans instead of work clothes makes me feel great. I remember how he held me that night in auto shop after Charles had been taken away and how, even then, I knew I'd be all right.

"The car's parked in front. Get your things loaded." He gives a Virgo scrunch of the nose at the mess. "We leave in an hour."

That's right. In just one hour, we will be on our way to Monterey. My mom is going to fly in and meet us for dinner. It's a long trip, but then she loves to travel.

I'm packing and repacking the boxes when I hear a chime and look down at my phone. A text message from Nathan.

im sry

me 2

A short exchange and, I suspect, a final one. Chili, Paige, and I saw Geneva and him in the Honda yesterday. I don't know if this text message is a response to that or to the entire sad situation.

Geneva and Nathan. That's what had me so depressed right before I first found the book. All I'd wished for then was the fellowship, for Nathan to notice me, and for a butt like Geneva's. And at various times, I got everything except the butt.

Paige and Chili wanted to make the drive with us, but they had to leave last night for a week at the Chiliderians' cabin at the lake. Only slightly smaller than their house, the so-called cabin will be full of the smell of pine trees and Stella's wonderful food. I feel a tiny pang of sadness. This will be the first year I'm not going with them.

"We all got what we wanted most," Chili said as Paige and I helped her pack yesterday. "And that's because of *Fearless Astrology*."

"Or maybe just because we're fearless," I said.

"Or a little less fearful than we used to be," Paige said in that scholarly way of hers.

Trevor has already asked if he can visit Chili at the lake. Whatever he had with Kat is definitely over. When they return, Paige (and Calypso, of course) will start a summer design course at the junior college.

Hunter will be taking summer courses there as well. I was totally wrong about him, totally wrong. Just because he has an Aries Sun, and because of my negative Aries experience with Kat, I jumped to all kinds of conclusions. He's a good guy, and the only reason he sometimes misses work at the coffee shop is because he works late at his other jobs.

There's still so much for me to try to figure out, like Moon signs for instance, and how they color and influence a person's Sun. Like Venus and Mars, and Geneva, for that matter. If we're supposed to be trined, why do we dislike each other so much?

She and Nathan were allowed to graduate, but I wasn't around to watch it. They have been a couple since the Gears were punished and Frankenstein announced that I had won the fellowship.

"Logan," my dad calls from the hall. "You need to get moving, honey."

Virgo translation: *Make the room look the way it did when you entered it.*

"I'm almost ready," I say.

But I can't help digging into one more box.

A photograph of my junior high school graduation falls out. There we are in our froufrou dresses. Paige and I looking scared, Chili looking perfect, all of us holding hands and daring the camera to capture us. I miss them already.

At the bottom of a yearbook box, I see the familiar tarnished twinkle. *Fearless Astrology, Volume II.* I start to shove it in my backpack and realize that Dad is standing in the doorway watching me.

"Busted," I say, and glance up at him, wondering how big a fit he's going to throw.

But the look I get from him is tender and a little embarrassed. "You come by it honestly, honey."

"What are you talking about?"

He steps inside and kneels beside me. "I should have told you sooner. My mom is J. Blair. She invented the last name because back then people would have thought she was weird for writing about astrology."

I stare at the book and try to process what he's just said. My hippified gram with her old-fashioned sayings and wild hair the color of mine?

"Gram Janie? She wrote this? Why did everyone keep it from me?"

"She and I had a disagreement having to do with what she

thought she saw in my chart," he says. "I'll tell you all about it later. For now, just let me say I was wrong to try to keep you away from her or the book."

"What changed your mind?" I ask.

"*You*, Logan." He gives me a hug, and I feel warm and secure in spite of all the crazy questions filling my head. "I've watched how you've changed this year, how confident you've become, and I've also come to terms with a lot of my own stuff."

"Thank you," I tell him. Then I grab the book and my bag and rush outside before I start to cry.

It's more dark than light out. Only a ghost moon glows in the gray-blue of the sky. The air is fresh with beginnings, still cool enough to make my skin prickle, but with the faint scent of the budding lilacs in the breeze.

Tonight I'll be in my new world. But for now, I just stand here with my bare feet on the cold concrete and watch this neighborhood I've grown up in as it awakens one more time around me.

I hear a noise, turn, and see my dad standing behind me at the front door.

"Ready?" he asks in a husky voice.

"I guess so."

I realize he's carrying my shoes and that he hasn't moved.

I walk over and take them from him, start to ask what's wrong. And then I see the streak of silver drive onto my street. I'm so shocked that it takes me a moment to process. The Spyder pulls into our driveway so fast that I jump out of the way. Chili and Paige, both of them in jeans, pile out and head for me. Stunned, I run to hug them.

"Mom postponed our vacation a week," Chili shouts.

"And she made shish kebab sandwiches and tabbouli salad for our lunch." Paige lets go of me long enough to open the back door of the Spyder, remove a huge foil-wrapped bundle, and hand it to my dad.

He puts it on the passenger seat of our car and then gets behind the wheel.

Chili throws her arm around me. "We are going to Monterey with you, babe," she says.

Still clutching my shoes, I climb into the backseat.

"You knew?" I ask my dad.

"Stella called when you were in the shower." He grins. "Who says a Virgo can't keep a secret?"

"That's because Virgos are helpful," I reply. "Sometimes, that is."

Chili and Paige slide in on either side of me, and the car fills with the smell of garlic.

The fellowship. I have the fellowship, and I am driving to Monterey with my two best friends. As we leave the neighborhood and head for the freeway, the sun begins to break through the dim light of the sky. Sitting between Paige and Chili, I watch the vineyards and the farms fly by.

"Hey, Astro Girl." Chili hugs me again. "What's in the stars for us?"

I hug her back and say, "Everything."

WHAT'S YOUR SUN SIGN?

SIX TRAITS EACH. REMEMBER, THE SUN IS NOT THE
SUM. IT IS ONLY THE BEGINNING.

—*Fearless Astrology*

Aries: **March 21–22 to April 19–20**

Energetic, Enthusiastic, Take-charge, Self-centered,
Quick-tempered, Aggressive, You value: Attention

Taurus: **April 20–21 to May 20–21**

Reliable, Kind-hearted, Sensuous, Stubborn,
Judgmental, Lazy, You value: Stability

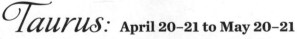

Gemini: **May 21–22 to June 21–22**

Strong communicator, Versatile, Generous, Fickle, Scattered, Nervous, You value: Intellect

Cancer: **June 22–23 to July 22–23**

Nurturing, Traditional, Family-oriented, Clingy, Codependent, Moody, You value: Empathy

Leo: **July 23–24 to Aug 23–24**

Leader, Full of fun, Warm and loving, Overbearing
Attention-seeking, Insensitive, You value: Creativity

Virgo: **Aug 23–24 to Sept 23–24**

Nitpicky, Helpful, Methodical, Shy, Critical,
Cheap, You value: Organization

Libra: **Sept 23–24 to Oct 23–24**

Attracted to beauty, Charming, Flexible, Wishy-washy
Manipulative, Jealous, You value: Fairness

Scorpio: **Oct 24–25 to Nov 21–22**

Intense, Passionate, Secretive, Compulsive
Sarcastic, Vindictive, You value: Loyalty

Sagittarius: **Nov 22–23 to Dec 21–22**

Optimistic, Goal-oriented, Independent, A loner

Restless, Blunt, You value: Adventure

Capricorn: **Dec 22–23 to Jan 19–20**

Hard-working, Disciplined, Trustworthy, Rigid, Dominating

Overly disciplined, You value: Determination

Aquarius: **Jan 20–21 to Feb 18–19**

Friendly, Caring, Humanitarian, Nonconformist
Eccentric, Just plain weird, You value: Humanity

Pisces: **Feb 19–20 to March 20–21**

Sensitive, Compassionate, Creative, Self-sacrificing
Dreamy, Introverted, You value: Imagination

HERE'S A SNEAK PEEK
AT THE NEXT BOOK IN THE
STAR CROSSED SERIES

TAURUS EYES

WELCOME TO FEARLESS ASTROLOGY, VOLUME 2. USE THE KNOWLEDGE THAT YOU GAIN HERE WISELY. IT WILL SERVE YOU WELL THROUGH TIMES OF JOY AND TIMES OF CHALLENGE.

—Fearless Astrology

The ghost tour leader was ten minutes late. I didn't care. Although I'd put on a good show, I, Logan McRae, was miserable. My mom had left for another golf tour. My two best girlfriends were on vacation. Worst of all, I'd lost a guy I really cared about, and in a very public way.

So, no, I wasn't all that interested in Monterey's ghosts, its Cannery Row or the tantalizing fragrance of the sea air.

Breaking up with someone you care about can do that to you. Times of challenge. You got that one right, *Fearless*.

I glanced up at the moon. It would be in the emotional sign of Cancer for another day-and-a-half. No way was I going to let that moon influence my wallowing. Time to focus on the good.

Here I was with a fellowship to the California State University at Monterey Bay for outstanding high school journalism students. My new roommate, Candice Armstrong, and I would soon join twelve other kids to take a tour of Monterey's supposedly haunted downtown. Our guest lecturer was none other than Henry Jaffa. *The* Henry Jaffa. Best-selling paranormal investigative journalist, who donated time and money to help young writers. That Henry Jaffa.

He had sat right across the table from me at dinner, and I'd barely been able to eat. All of us had just kept staring at him. Except for Vanessa Lowe, that is, a pushy, curvy brunette from Texas. She'd hammered him with questions and flattery from the clam chowder right through the halibut parmesan. She was still talking while Jaffa tried to swallow a few spoonfuls of his melting hazelnut gelato.

Candice and I stood together outside the restaurant waiting for the tour bus. We both wore jeans and our black T-shirts with Writers Camp in purple letters on the front. I had to admit neither of us filled them out the way Vanessa did hers.

Candice was about my size, except on her, thin looked good. She had shiny, streaked rich-girl hair and a way of carrying herself that made her appear taller than she was. In a word, she was elegant. A steady Earth sign, I guessed, with a cool exterior that made me guess Capricorn somewhere in her chart. Dirk, a cute British guy with a long ponytail, had been checking her out at dinner, but she told me she had a boyfriend back home in Colorado. She also had two older sisters, who were, she said, a royal pain. I had worried that I would get stuck with a Vanessa-type roommate and was glad that Candice seemed so calm and easygoing.

The two redheads from New York were twins and, of course, roomed together. Christopher Ritter, who introduced himself as Critter, was a stoner with blond curls and a laidback way of speaking that must have taken a lot of practice to pull off. I didn't have names for the others yet.

"Could you believe the wicked witch of west Texas?" Candice asked. "With Vanessa in the workshop, we'll be lucky to even talk to Jaffa."

"With him," I said. "I don't think it's about the talking."

Candice nodded. "It's about the writing. Let's hope she sucks at it."

"Or that she's easily distracted." On the other side of the walkway, Vanessa chatted up a cute guy in a khaki jacket with a matching bag over his shoulder. "If that guy's part of our workshop, she might not be that interested in Jaffa after all."

"He's cute, but he isn't a bestselling writer," Candice said.

"He is hot, though," I replied.

Just then, a dark green bus pulled up, and a woman with a gray bob stepped out. Her face was younger than her hair, her eyes hidden behind pink-tinted glasses.

"Writers Camp tour boarding now," she called out in a starched, professional voice. "We leave in ten minutes. Mr. Jaffa, please come forward."

Jaffa emerged from the crowd and climbed up the stairs.

The cute guy was next. Then came the African American chick who'd sat on the other side of Jaffa at dinner. As she swung up the steps to the bus, her violet tie-dyed scarf blew behind her. It matched the streak of hair falling over one eye.

"Let's go," Candice said, and we began to run.

She got there first. Then, finally, I was aboard. Ahead of me, Henry Jaffa sat next to a window paging through a guidebook. His bushy gray hair caught the lights of the bus. The seat beside him was empty. This was my chance. I started toward him.

Then I felt someone hit me from behind. In the back. Hard.

As I fought to maintain my balance, Vanessa gave me a final shove, pushed ahead of me, and claimed the seat beside Jaffa.

A hand on the other side of the aisle shot out and grabbed mine. I looked up into riveting eyes the color of the sea. The noise of the others blurred into a steady hum. It was the cute guy who'd been talking to Vanessa outside.

He was about my age with hair so straight and shiny black that I immediately thought about my own auburn curls, no doubt hopelessly frizzed by the sea air. Although our connection must have lasted only moments, time stretched out. Then slowly, he pulled me down in the seat next to him.

Finally, the sound in my head switched back on. I heard the chatter of the others and was able to remove my hand from his.

"Thank you," I said. "I guess I tripped." The words fell out of me clunky and stupid.

"What's your name?"

"Logan."

"I'm Jeremy." His voice was husky, yet soft. "Jeremy Novack."

"And you're part of the Writers Camp too?"

He opened his jacket, pointed at his shirt, identical to mine. "My plane was late. I just got in."

"Where are you from?"

"Jersey," he said. "I'm sorry I missed the dinner, but I can't believe I bothered to show up for this sham."

"They're doing it because Jaffa's next book is going to be about ghost sightings," I said.

"He needs to stick to the investigative stuff. You don't believe any of the ghost stories are real, do you?"

"I don't know." Those eyes of his made it almost impossible for me to remember my name, let alone anything else.

"It's hype."

Taurus. He had to be that fixed Bull of the Zodiac. I could guess his opinion of astrology.

The silver-haired tour guide stepped inside the bus.

"Is everyone aboard? Our first stop will be a bar and

restaurant that has two ghosts."

Jeremy sighed.

Ahead and to the other side of us, I watched Jaffa nod. Beside him, Vanessa paged through what looked like a well used booklet. She'd obviously done her Monterey-lore homework.

"Big deal," Jeremy whispered to me. "All that stuff's easy to fake."

"The female ghost at the restaurant leaves salt in the wineglasses," Vanessa piped up.

Jaffa looked intrigued. "Monterey is full of legends and mysteries," he said. "That's one of the reasons I agreed to come here."

"Sean Baylor is another one." Vanessa glanced up from her book with a superior smile. "He was a folk singer who almost made it big in the late sixties. Some believe his spirit still occupies the restaurant where he drank before he went out on his boat that last time after the Monterey Pop Festival."

"There's no proof that Baylor is a ghost," Jeremy said. Then to me, he whispered, "Do you see what I mean about this stuff?"

Before I could reply, the tour guide said, "Well, his sailboat was found deserted in a storm. There's no way he could have survived."

"So that means he decided to stick around and haunt old Monterey?"

The woman flashed him a condescending smile. "There's no way we can know which spirits remain, or why. And, for your information, this is one of the most popular walking tours in Monterey."

"Well, have fun with your popular walking tour." He stood, said "Nice meeting you, Logan," stepped across me, and headed down the aisle toward the door.

"Wait," our tour guide shouted as he brushed past her. "This bus leaves in five minutes. It isn't going to wait for you."

"That's all right." He looked back at me again. I felt the connection and realized I couldn't stay in my seat.

"Logan," Candice called from behind me. "What are you doing?"

"I'll be right back," I said. Then I hurried past the guide, got off the bus, and started after him.

"Jeremy, wait."

He stopped and turned his head. He gave me that look again. "You'd better get back on the bus."

"Not without you," I said. "I know how hard you must have worked to get this fellowship. How can you walk away from it? How can you walk away from Henry Jaffa?"

He pulled his jacket closer and met my gaze. "I can walk away from anyone, if I have to."

I felt a chill and forced myself to ignore his words. "But you don't have to. Please come back on that bus with me."

"No way. I have to check in at the college, and I'm up to here with the ghost stuff."

"All right. If that's the way you want it." I felt like a fool for chasing after him. Slowly, I turned away. This was the smartest thing I'd done all day. Just walk back to the bus.

"Logan, don't go."

He was right behind me. I could feel his breath on my neck.

I whirled around and found myself face-to-face with him. "What?"

For the first time since he'd grabbed my hand back in the bus, he smiled.

"Let's ditch the tour and get something to eat."

"I can't."

"Why not?"

Because Henry Jaffa was on that bus. Because the beginning of the fellowship I'd fought like hell for was on that bus. Because regardless of how hot Jeremy was, I couldn't blow my dream.

"I'm sorry," I said. "I really wish . . ."

"Three minutes," announced the tour guide. She'd stepped outside the bus and was glaring at us now. "Two minutes, forty-five seconds. Are you two boarding, or would you like to walk back to the college?"

"I'll walk," Jeremy shouted back at her.

I ran for the bus.

The doors whooshed shut behind me.

The bus driver hit the gas, and I had to grab the back of his seat to steady myself. Our guide slid behind him. I made my way to the seats Jeremy and I had occupied earlier. When I saw his empty one next to the window, I felt unreasonably sad.

I'd made the right choice, though. This fellowship could change my life. I looked up to where Henry Jaffa sat. It was only then that I realized that Vanessa was still occupying the outside seat. She gave me a smirk and then she turned back to Jaffa.

Oh great. My first night in Monterey, and I already had an enemy.

Notes to Self

For some reason, Vanessa hates me. When we had to introduce ourselves on the bus and tell where we were from, she made fun of my answer. I'd said Terra Bella Beach and explained it was about ninety minutes south between here and Santa Barbara. "I can tell you're from California, Logan," she'd said with a condescending smile. "You give directions by how long it takes to get to a place." I didn't like the way she looked at me; I didn't like the laughter of the others. I especially didn't like that Jeremy wasn't in the seat beside me. So, yes, I have an enemy, a Fire sign, I'll bet. Tomorrow is our first day in class, and I'd better be ready for her.

Hamlet Was a Libra

"To be or not to be?" With all of his wondering and all of his questioning, Hamlet had to be a Libra. They frequently have trouble making up their minds. His love for beauty—think Ophelia—is par for the course for one ruled by Venus. There's a lot of talk from this Air sign, too, and Libras are known for their communication skills.

I stop writing. The talk could also mean that Hamlet was a Gemini or even a Sadge. And with all of that karmic family emotional stuff, he could have been a Scorpio or a Cancer. The emoting on stage could be the sign of a Leo or Aries. Many Capricorns have unsettled childhoods. He certainly qualified in that department. Then, there are emotionally stuck Pisces, pondering Aquarius, perfectionist Virgo, anduncompromising Taurus. When I first discovered *Fearless Astrology*, I would have made that easy assumption about Libra. Now I realize that what I need to do with my article is to show how the Sun sign is really only the beginning. Yes. Instead of trying to argue the sign of a fictional character, I'm going to show how impossible it is to use only the Sun to understand someone, fictional or otherwise.

Jaffa is known for his interest in subjects off the beaten track. I can't wait to see what he thinks about astrology.

Bonnie Hearn Hill is a Gemini and a full-time writer and a former editor for a daily newspaper. She is the author of INTERN and five other adult thriller novels, and teaches writing in her hometown of Fresno, California and on Writer's Digest Online. She also mentors writers and speaks at numerous writing conferences. Read more about Bonnie and your astrological sign at: www.bonniehearnhill.com